A great many thoughts and emotions were building up inside me. One moment I was dissing gays in my mind and in another I was actually defending them. By dissing them, I was in touch with the male part of me that popular society wanted to emphasize. Since popular society never held much regard for me, I refused to hold much regard for it.

This, in turn, allowed me to explore other areas of deep thought. If there is or ever could be such a thing as a bottomless cup of coffee. Why people called it rush hour when nothing moved. Just how many licks does it take to get to the center of a Tootsie Roll Pop. Women still counted as a mystery, and probably would in any century. They were still a mystery to me, at least.

What did they think about me? That I was a geek? A few maybe thought I was a gay geek. Why did they think I was...that way? That really pissed me off! Just because I didn't go out every weekend and pick up some woman to have sex with or hit on someone at work during the week and use her to warm up for the weekend, suddenly I'm gay? I don't think so.

A FUNNY THING HAPPENED
ON THE WAY TO MY
SEXUAL
ORIENTATION

KAGE ALAN

ZUMAYA BOUNDLESS   AUSTIN TX

2008

This book is a work of fiction. Names, characters, places and incidents are products of the author's imagination or are used fictitiously. Any resemblance to actual persons or events is purely coincidental.

A FUNNY THING HAPPENED ON THE WAY TO MY
SEXUAL ORIENTATION
© 2008 by Kage Alan

ISBN 978-1-934135-91-4

Cover art and design by Angela Waters

Zumaya Boundless is an imprint of Zumaya Publications LLC, Austin TX. Look for us online at http://www.zumayapublications.com

Library of Congress Cataloging-in-Publication Data

Alan, Kage, 1970-
    A funny thing happened on the way to my sexual
    orientation / Kage Alan.
        p. cm.
ISBN 978-1-934135-91-4 (alk. paper)
1. Gay college students--Fiction. 2. Coming out (Sexual orientation)--Fiction. 3. California--Fiction. I. Title.
PS3601.L327F86 2008
813'.6--dc22
                                        2008028033

For Ralph,
Who with three words
changed my life.

I love you
forever and always...

5-30-09

To the polite, dapper and
handsome Gary!
How was that?
Many thanx for taking an
interest in the books.
Enjoy,
Kage Alan

Special Thanks To: My parents for *everything* (love, support, editing skills and believing in me), Tashka, Kira and Jesse.

Thanks To: Milt Ford, Sharon Whitehill, Diane Abbott, Don Zomberg, Jay Taylor, Jose Reyes, Chad Voelkers, Jack Cain, Anthony Seaman, Greg Sievert, Chester Swider, Amy Fletemier, Sue Kenty-Roberts, Theresa Taylor, Todd Miller, Jennifer Neault, the Grand Valley State University Tutoring Center 1989-1993 and Gladys Hurst.

Thanks To Those Whom I've Never Met But Who Inspired This Work Nonetheless: Marian Gold, Roland Orzabal, Curt Smith, Per Gessle, Marie Fredriksson, Michael Cretu, Vangelis, Hans Zimmer, Martha Davis and Jordan Young.

FOREWORD

Having your first novel published is an exhilarating time, but more work than you can possibly imagine. Unless you're a household name or been featured on *Oprah*, get ready to learn the fine art of PR: how to find all the cheap flights, cheap hotels, cheap transportation to and from the cheap flights and cheap hotels, make contacts at bookstores, keep the stores in touch with their distributors, keep the distributors in touch with your publisher, keep in touch with all the publications who might review your work, pray people will show up to your signings, rely on your friends' unique talents that you never realized they had and hope to heck your book was worth all the trouble you went through in the end anyway.

Still sound easy? Then try dealing with a New York cab driver...because that's *fun*.

There wouldn't have been a release of *A Funny Thing...* if I didn't have the complete support of my partner, and there wouldn't have been a new edition without the support of my family, friends (both new and old) and new publisher. I humbly thank you all. I also thank you for your continued interest in my work. There's plenty left to share, so strap yourselves in.

Having said that, let's get on with the Version 2.0 of *A Funny Thing...* featuring:

- All new special effects!
- A new cover!
- Fewer typos!
- A new surprise or two!
- Subliminal messages suggesting you also buy the sequel, *Andy Stevenson vs. The Lord of the Loins*!

Sincerely,

Kage Alan

November 8, 2007

INTRO

Love is a phenomenal experience. For some, it's merely a passing fanny while for others, like myself, it is the end of a long and often painful, if not embarrassing, journey into adulthood.

I used to find it difficult to believe in true romantic love the way I found it difficult to believe in God, mostly because I'd never experienced either—or thought I hadn't, in the case of God. Now—*now*—I believe in miracles and God because of love, but it didn't start out that way, not even close.

It seems ironic to me now that I never caught on to all the signs about my sexuality that appeared to me early on in life. Then again, maybe it isn't so ironic after all, especially with the way society feels about gays. I think I was too young to understand names and labels and religious beliefs dictating right from wrong in areas where only a fundamental fear of the unknown existed. It's universal for people to fear and lash out against what they don't understand. Homosexuality is no exception. Of course, rap music wasn't accepted by society for a while either, so maybe there's hope after all.

The only unknown mysteries in life that I cared about back when I was growing up were what episodes of *Johnny Sokko & His Flying Robot*, *Ultraman* and *Battlestar Galactica* were going to be on TV that week. A few years after that, the mystery of what made my body feel good became a fixation, as it did for many other boys my age. However, that's said to be natural and normal, and experimentation can be chalked up to boys just being boys. No harm is really done, as long as it doesn't continue past a certain age where those curiosities are supposed to end and new ones begin.

That new age of curiosities was when I think I began to run into trouble, because the old one never quit. I still somehow managed to repress acting them out and tried to focus on women instead. Essentially, that went nowhere. The harder I tried to make myself interested in the opposite sex, the further I distanced myself from everybody, include-ing myself, and I was only in junior high at the time!

My true search for love, that one thing I'd never had or felt before, didn't begin until after my first year of college while on a trip to California. I don't think I was really ready to begin my quest before then, and I certainly wasn't prepared for what I found. The sum of my experiences early on in life forced me to reach out and become someone I had the potential to be, as opposed to the wisecracking smartass I was; but in doing so, it also forced me to come to terms with my true sexuality.

Who knew that my life would change forever in the space of six days?

1

Hi. My name's Andy. Not Andrew or anything foreign, just Andy. It isn't the greatest name in the world, but it certainly isn't the worst. My parents liked the sound of it, but I prefer to think that I was intentionally named after Andy Taylor, the really cool Duran Duran ex-guitarist. There are certainly worse people and worse things to be named after. I knew a kid from Illinois whose name was John. Not Jonathan, just John. He swore up and down that his parents wanted a daughter and named him after a urinal out of spite. His parents were bitter that way. Still, John had to admit that things could have been worse. Neither one of us is named Richard.

When I think about how things started, I don't believe I wanted to "come out" at all. I wasn't happy, and in all honesty, I wasn't exactly the most likeable person at times; but that didn't bother me as much as having to admit to myself that I was gay. I couldn't do it, maybe because I equated it with finding out from the doctor that I had some nasty disease, that I was going to be branded by society as an undesirable and be a victim for the rest of my life.

Nevertheless, slowly but surely, I came to the realization that I was, indeed, gay; and it didn't seem nearly as bad as I'd first thought. Wasn't I still the same sarcastic son of a bitch, if not a bit happier? Wasn't I looking for someone to share my life with and wake up next to in the morning on a more permanent basis? Wouldn't it be nice if they remembered my name for a change? And didn't I want to live beyond my meager means and pay for everything by credit card?

Yes! I wanted all the things that every hetero-sexual male did, so imagine the irony I felt when I was branded by society as an undesirable and had to fight to not be a victim anyway. Funny how that works, isn't it? Yeah, well, so is Viagra.

A lot of straight people wonder how someone "becomes" gay, or if they were really born that way or even if it has something to do with their environment.

Good questions.

I'm an only child, and I have always been close to both my parents. I wasn't sexually abused and never lusted after my mother. For that matter, I never lusted after my father. I really didn't need to say that, but it never ceases to amaze me what questions people will actually think of when there's a gay man or woman around.

Let me just get some of the answers to standard questions out of the way now. I don't molest children. I don't look at guys in the shower. I don't stare at guys' crotches at the gym, and I don't walk into a room and start picking out guys to try and seduce. Ideas like that only add to existing problems and misconceptions about gays.

I was never big into sports, but I did enjoy reading and playing with my Legos, *Star Wars* toys and Atari video games. This seems to be a pretty normal childhood to me. I do have a number of cousins on both sides of my family who are gay, only I wasn't aware of it back then. Heck, I never even met them, since they lived out in California and my grandparents never spoke about them.

In light of all this, I find it difficult to believe that I was somehow "influenced to become gay."

One final idea that straight people have about gays is that they're looking for acceptance of some kind, and that ultimately steers them into homosexuality. Yeah, right. Ultimate acceptance through ultimate disapproval? And a sane person thought this up?

What I can tell you about my childhood is that I liked having friends who were girls. I've always felt comfortable talking to women, and tended to make a better friend than date. Too, I liked having guy friends, and I can remember pursuing friendships with guys who I found to be attractive and wanted to experiment with, even as far back as grade school. Kids are curious at that age, only I was *really* curious.

There was Jim in third grade, Andrew in fourth, Scott and Mike in fifth and Randy in sixth. With my blue eyes and blond hair, they weren't too difficult to convince. Still, I was too young to be called a slut and too stupid to realize what this was all pointing to.

I had two more experiences, one in eighth grade and another in ninth, and then it ended. Most of the people I'd had these experiences with had moved away by the time I entered tenth grade, so I wasn't in too much danger of my classmates finding out. I was still worried, though. The mere possibility of being found out was enough to make me insecure and an easy target to abusive peers.

Just to be on the safe side, I did date girls during those years to make it look like I was "normal." I started dating a girl when I was a sophomore who was genuinely special and who treated me very, very well. I can remember riding my bike over to her house a number of times and watching a movie or playing on the computer with her. When we weren't together, we talked on the phone for hours, and it didn't matter what we were talking about as long as we were talking. At school, I met her each day at her locker and then between classes, when the rooms were actually close enough. I was, in essence, everything the perfect boyfriend was supposed to be, and she was everything the perfect girlfriend was supposed to be.

I began to worry as the relationship progressed toward where it would inevitably lead. We liked each other well enough, but there were some deeper desires that seemed to be awakening in her that never woke up in me. I was scared to death to tell her that I was attracted to her in every way except sexually, and the closer she tried to get, the further I pushed her away. I think she thought I might have been a bit of a prude, but I didn't have to worry about it very long. In the end, she decided she wasn't going to wait around for me to lose my morality...and virginity. She had a new boyfriend within a few weeks who had her in bed experimenting with handcuffs and flavored lubricants.

I was so shattered from losing the closeness I had shared with her that I didn't date again until I was a senior. Even then, that relationship only lasted a few weeks before I got dumped for a pizza boy. He was apparently willing to deliver the kind of pepperoni I wasn't.

Suffice to say that neither of these experiences did much for my self-esteem.

Dating was just entirely too depressing to deal with after that. The loneliness and bouts of depression were worse some months than others, but I got through it and graduated. Most of the four hundred students in my class could have gone to hell, and it never would have fazed me. In fact, I often told them to, since I was also known for being a smart-ass.

I have a very simple philosophy about this matter: I was born a dumbass, have since become a smartass and one day aspire to be a wiseass. It used to get me into a lot of trouble because my comments bordered on downright cruelty and bad taste, but that was because I was using them to cover up my own insecurities by exposing others'. I wanted to be nicer, but it's just that there wasn't a great deal of opportunity for a person to change or evolve into someone other than what one's peers perceived them to be. That's why I was looking forward to college so much.

While others went off to places like Michigan State, U of M, Western, Eastern, a few to Northern—nobody ever seemed to go to Southern— I chose a university in the cornfields. My reasoning for this was simple; there was a smaller student-to-teacher ratio than at the elite schools and my parents had met there. They weren't such bad people, so maybe I could straighten my life out there like they had, come to my senses and find some nice young woman to settle down with.

Unfortunately, aside from that motive, I really didn't have much of an idea of what I wanted to do professionally. I wondered if procrastination was a major. Well, that decision could wait.

Another thing I didn't realize was that I was moving to an area of west Michigan termed "the Bible belt," and the people in this churchgoing farming area disliked sinning college students, which was basically all college students in their minds, alcoholic beverages other than the wine at church, stores open on Sunday, people doing work on Sunday, and McDonalds.

Why McDonalds? Well, it went like this. The people in the little town where the university was located fought to keep all fast food restaurants from within their city limits because they felt it would bring the town down. Apparently, eating fast food meant one had fast morals. I would have thought that after smelling cowshit for an entire day, a Big Mac would really have hit the spot, but apparently I was misguided.

McDonalds just happened to be the one franchise being persistent in trying to obtain a permit. In response, the townspeople started a boycott against this heathen chain. Like that was really going to hurt them.

The first semester of my freshman year turned out to be hell. I was homesick, my roommate was rarely around, I was still in denial, and I ended up on academic probation because I failed chemistry. Oh, yeah, now, *there's* a worthwhile class. It ranks right up there with "Theories of Adult Pornographic Videos." I would no more sit down with friends and discuss why the director chose a specific noir lighting technique on the woman's breasts than I would what the delta heat of some varying degree on a stalactite might be.

Between that class and others, figuring out a major and listening to the preachers who roamed the campus telling us all that we needed to be saved, I didn't have much time to think about romance or even sexuality in general.

On a positive note, I did take my first writing class. Dr. Lockman essentially geared it towards working on smaller essays about ourselves and then combining them to create a single autobiography. I hated English, and had low self-esteem, so imagine the pleasure I derived from writing about myself.

I did learn three major things in that class. First, what a comma looks like and how to use one; second, that I had been taught how to write a paragraph incorrectly in high school and third, that I really could write. In a sea of core classes designed to give me a well-rounded education, like chemistry, I discovered that I not only enjoyed writing but was fairly good at it, too.

Before the semester ended, Dr. Lockman recommended that I jump a level and take a literature class instead of another "write a new paper each week" class. His enthusiasm and support convinced me it was the way to go. I finally had some direction.

❦ ❦ ❦

Second semester was much better than the first. I started going out to see comedians, movies and concerts the University sponsored. Hell, I was even social and talked to someone next to me once in a while. Aside from that, I also began writing a music column for the campus newspaper. It didn't pay much and the hate mail was considerable, but I was writing and expressing myself in a rather uncensored and often unpopular fashion. I didn't have a great deal of money to go out every week and buy a new album, but it was easy to tell what people were listening to, since one could rarely sleep during the weekends with the sound systems blaring to cover up the number of one-night stands going on. I just listened to what they played.

As for sexual encounters of the college kind, the guys on my floor were particularly notorious for that sort of thing. All they had to do was look at a girl once, and they could tell what kind of night she was going to have. My notes on their pickup lines and nonverbal methods of communication are extensive.

The lit class Dr. Lockman suggested I take turned out to be one of the best classes I could have taken to continue my interest in writing. The catalogue listed our professor's name as "Staff," which of course just meant they hadn't assigned an instructor yet. The man who walked through the door that first meeting was a kindly gentleman in his forties who seemed very open to different interpretations of literature and writing. Much to our amazement, the name on the syllabus he passed out was, indeed, "Professor Staff", which meant he either had a sense of humor or that was actually his name.

Either way, he had us all wondering, and I received my first look at his true colors a few weeks later when he was handing back our first papers. A group of us had been slaving over them for two weeks, helping each other as much as we could and really looking forward to seeing our grades. Wasn't that stupid?

My paper was on William Wordsworth. The Professor, as he politely insisted we call him, passed my desk and handed me my paper with a twinkle in his eye. The moment had arrived, and considering the look he gave me, the prospects for a decent grade looked fantastic. There in my hand lay the fruits of my labor for the past two weeks. Here was where my writing would really take off!

I took a long, deep breath and flipped to the last page. A few comments were written down...blah blah blah...There it was! Or, rather, there it was.

I felt my stomach drop and my lip curl. B-minus. Wasn't that quaint?

"Son of a bitch," I muttered. My own mother would have been hard-pressed to hear me, and she'd had years of practice.

"Andy?" The Professor was looking at me. "Why don't you stay after class, and we'll talk about your grade?"

I couldn't believe he heard me! It was both unexpected and unsettling—mostly unsettling— and I thought about just how good a chemistry class would be right now compared to the horror of having been heard swearing by the man who made or broke my grade.

Bile rose up in my throat on more than one

occasion, and my stomach began doing flip-flops while I was waiting for class to end. The minutes passed by with my insides in agony until it was finally time to leave. Maybe I could play like I was stupid or an inbred child from the South here on a scholarship. Hey, they gave them to everybody else. Just the other day I'd seen a kid who couldn't even spell his name, and he had a scholarship.

Of course, my roommate told me later the kid was dyslexic. Apparently, there weren't enough minority students enrolled at the university with that ethnic background. Still, just because he has a foreign heritage didn't mean he couldn't learn how to spell.

"I take it you weren't happy with your grade?" The Professor looked at me with kind eyes. If he was upset or angry, it didn't show.

"I was just kind of surprised. A group of us worked together pretty hard, and I thought I'd done better." So much for the inbred act. "It, uh, probably wasn't the ideal paper for straight-up, cut-and-dried factual statements with appropriate ob-servations in the analytical style and accepted APA format, but that's because I hate writing something dull and didactic. I end up adding personal com-mentary but tried to keep it from influencing or hampering the general narrative structure too much."

For God's sake, I was practically giving him the formula for glue instead of just telling him that I liked to make quirky little comments for no good reason other than for my own entertainment.

"Well, I want you to know that I can appreciate that kind of writing, and I think commentary does liven up a piece, but you should also know that there are going to be instructors here who don't."

He paused as if pondering whether he should say anything further. At least I felt like we were making some kind of one-on-one connection. How many students at Michigan State could say their instructors knew their name?

"If you would like, I'd be willing to help you develop your writing skills for this and other classes so you could get away with what you're doing."

I was starting to like him.

"You have some talent in writing, but it's raw yet. You need to strengthen and hone it, though. If you want."

I did.

The rest of the conversation was uninspiring, but I left with a really good feeling. My stomach wasn't acting up like it had before our talk, and for the first time, I was starting to see the possibility of being adopted by someone who would act as my mentor and guide me in the strange and mystical ways of the Writer. Or whatever.

It was back to beating chemistry again.

❀ ❀ ❀

I went from there over to the Commons, and after an extremely unsatisfying dinner to the campus library. I doubt I will ever forget how exhilarating it is to smell the scent of freshly thawed fertilizer wafting over the campus from the neighboring fields. Expressing my gratitude to Mother Nature for this unusually warm day wouldn't have come out very nicely.

Then too, there is a saying in Michigan: "If you

don't like the weather, just wait five minutes." It's true, and at least I now knew the reason my roommate had asked me to look up some topic for him that he had to write a paper on. I think he was still probably enjoying his dinner at Burger King or wherever in Grand Rapids he went, wonderfully ignorant of what I was going through.

Since the computer system in the library was probably the quickest and most convenient way of looking up my roommate's subject, I found a machine that wasn't occupied and sat down. I typed in "Youths in Asia," and when the computer came back with "No Subject Found" I typed it in again anyway in case it was mistaken. It wasn't. I tried every single spelling combination I could think of until I was a smelly, sweating ball of frustration. Why was it so damn difficult? I mean, what the hell did Asia call its youth, anyway?

It followed that Asians would be found in Asia, not like that entire Canada/Canadian thing a friend played with my mind about. Because of her, I could never keep them straight. Basically, she told me that if I went to Canada the people there would be called Canadans. Consequently, if I was among Canadians, wouldn't I have traveled to Canadia?

This is one of those reasons my parents tried to dissuade me from drinking at college. They knew that, with the friends I had, my young and naive existence would be confusing enough without alcohol.

I ended up leaving in disgust and headed back to my dorm.

❦ ❦ ❦

Why some parents ever complained about guys and girls living together in the same dorm building is beyond me. It wasn't like we were on the same floor and sharing showers and bathrooms or anything like that. Large metal doors separated the two sexes at all times.

Granted, that never really seemed to matter when it came time for the two sexes to partake in a little sex, but that's beside the point for the moment.

Guys and girls living together created a balance. One floor smelled like old sweat socks mixed with Old Spice and the next like perfume and potpourri room fresheners. One floor looked like the remnant of a World War II battlefield and the next the Rainbow Bridge. The whole thing evened out, and I came to think of it as like the collegiate version of yin and yang. Of course, the guys were constantly trying to stick their yang in every girl's yin.

Then too, many of the girls were using their yin to get all the cute guys' yang. This effectively cut me out of the entire rat race, as I was neither interested in any girl's yin nor good-looking enough, in my opinion, at least, to attract one. I was also resolved to ignore any impulse towards any guy's yang. Again, it was a strange balance.

The lobby of the dorm was a flurry of activity when I walked in. Going on were some intense study groups in one of the well-lit alcoves, drug deals being made in the dimly lit one, three guys bragging about a recent female score and realizing they'd all had the same girl one right after the other, a resident assistant complaining to the building manager about a dead rabbit found impaled on his door with a hunting knife, two people bitching about the latest music review in the paper, seven people trying to get the combination locks undone on their mailbox and one girl on the phone bragging to her friend that she had just slept with three guys one right after the other and, unbeknownst to them, given them crabs.

I didn't know how I wanted to remember my college years, but this definitely wasn't it. There was no way I could blend in with these people, at least not at this stage of my life. Hell, I was still a virgin, and it wasn't as if I wanted to be one. It's just that I never went out of my way in the past to make myself physically desirable, like Fabio, so why should I do it now?

It had occurred to me that if someone was going to like me, then they should like me for who I really was. While I thought that was a very solid and honest philosophy to live by, it certainly didn't get me many dates or even much interest. In fact, it made me wonder whatever happened to my charm, or at least the persuasive nature I'd had in grade school through the first part of high school. Of course, that was with guys, and that time of my life was forever over with.

Truth be told, I guess I was still a bit curious about other guys but decided to keep it to myself, since that kind of curiosity was no longer considered innocent. Hell, it could get the crap kicked out of me, and that thought alone was enough to make me continue burying my feelings. Weren't there people out there who remained curious, too? Was I the exception to the rule in still being who I was while having these feelings?

I certainly didn't resemble in any way the kind of stereotypical "fag" used as the butt of a ton of tasteless jokes, so I couldn't be one. This was fine by me because I liked being who I was, the type of person I had potential to become; and there was no room in my life to be one of those limp-wristed, lisping, feminine-looking and acting queers laughed about and resented so openly. If that's what being gay was all about, then I wanted no part of it.

I didn't want any part of it anyway. I might not yet know exactly who I was, but I did know who I wasn't. My uncertainty about sex merely stemmed with never having been with a woman. Once that happened, I would come to my senses. It was just that simple, or so I thought.

My head hurt, and I wanted a shower more than anything else. I wanted to step under the rush of hot water and feel all the negative thoughts and energy wash from my body and disappear down the moldy drain on its way to the Commons. There was too much negativity in the world. Society needed to be a little more nurturing, a bit more caring. People needed to be a little kinder and respectful to each other.

"You smell like shit," Todd, my Neanderthal and negative roommate informed me matter-of-factly when I unlocked the door and stepped into the small dorm room.

"Oh, bite me."

Todd laughed and tossed me a bag of cold onion rings from Burger King. Actually, he wasn't so bad, and I'm not saying that just because he brought me food. Most of the time, one never knows what kind of person he or she will be paired up with in a dorm. I lucked out because Todd respected my privacy and the items I had brought with me from home as I respected his. We got along well enough, too, since we were different enough to make for some interesting conversations and alike enough not to argue over what to watch on TV. Sometimes I proofed or wrote some of his papers, and he paid for a movie in Grand Rapids or bought me a CD. He got what he needed, and I got what I wanted. It was a beneficial arrangement. The food he brought didn't hurt my opinion of him, either.

"I hope you earned the onion rings," he wondered out loud and pointed to my backpack. "What did you find?"

"You may want them back." I offered him the bag. "Because I couldn't find a thing."

He declined.

"The computer didn't have anything on them."

"Them?" Todd looked at me, confused. "What do you mean *them*?"

"Well..." I rolled my eyes. "...the youth in Asia or youths in Asia. Hello?"

Sometimes, he was a bit slow.

"I mean, I tried every combination, but it either told me there was nothing to be found or that I needed to narrow my search."

"Youths in Asia?" He was staring at me in disbelief.

"Uh, I think I just said that." I didn't feel so bad about eating his onion rings now. Sometimes I had to talk very slowly and in small words to get him to understand something. "Which part didn't you understand?"

"Which part didn't *you* understand?" he count-

16

ered. "I said *euthanasia*."

"Youth in Asia, youths in Asia, what's the difference? I still came up empty."

Todd put his hand up to his forehead in a mock gesture of surrendering to an idiot.

"What?"

"E-u-t-h-a-n-a-s-i-a." He spelled it out for me.

"Euthanasia?" I spoke the word out loud, and he nodded. "Well, what the hell is that?"

"That..." Todd smirked at me. "...is what I needed you to find out. Didn't you ask one of the librarians for help?"

"Huh?" Was he kidding? I stared at him and shoved two more onion rings into my mouth. It was hard to tell at this point which one of us was the bigger moron. At least neither one of us knew what euthanasia was, so in my mind, that made him the more moronic. From his view, I suspected, I should have known what it was, since I generally prided myself on knowing more than he did. That, in *his* mind, made me the more moronic one.

The only thing we would agree on is that we would disagree, so it was stupid for either of us to continue the conversation.

"You had a call earlier. Some girl." His voice was even, as if relating events that occurred regularly.

"Really?" It was a rather unusual occurrence. A girl calling me? It had a nice ring to it. There was a girl in Professor Staff's class named Tina who was pretty cute—blonde, nice green eyes, pleasant voice, great body, vacant look on her face, perfect sorority material. What the hell would she be doing calling me? "What did she want?"

"Just to say that your latest music review sucks,

Roxette sucks and, according to her, you do, too." He paused as if in deep thought. "She didn't leave a name or number."

It definitely wasn't Tina.

❦ ❦ ❦

Classes came and went daily, and homework took up a sizable chunk of time during the week, but that was mostly because I didn't want to do any of it on the weekend. I probably should have saved some of it because I tended not to do much on the weekend anyway.

My writing really started showing signs of improvement, and I was aching to try my pencil at some short stories and maybe even a novel. My other classes went well, and I knew that I was in no danger of being on academic probation again. The dean might not know my name yet, but the expulsion committee wouldn't, either. It was a fair trade. All I had to concentrate on now was finals.

Todd's finals finished on a Tuesday and mine that Wednesday. He was moved out an hour after his last exam but came back the next evening so the two of us could get drunk together before moving on to "greener pastures." He called it that because he was from the west side of the state and really was moving back to fields and pastures and all that farmer stuff.

That last night I spent with Todd was very special. He was extremely patient and gentle with me, especially since it was my first time—getting drunk, that is. When I could no longer feel my legs, he let me put my arm around his neck for support while I puked. When I could no longer feel the rest of my body, he held my head up so I didn't make a mess on the floor.

My parents arrived the next morning, but Todd had already left. I vaguely recall through my stupor a death threat if I ever became a writer and wrote about him unless it was published in *Penthouse*.

Mom and Dad were both happy to see me and glad I was confident I hadn't flunked out of school and wasted all their money. Aside from inquiring about my exams, the only questions they had were why I insisted that they speak very quietly and why they had to leave the "damn" curtains closed.

After all my stuff was safely packed away in the van, I went back upstairs for one last look around the room. So much had happened and changed since I'd first arrived. God only knew what would happen in the fall, but before I could get to that, I had to survive the summer.

2

Most people my age love the summertime. I hate it! I never went away and vacationed in some distant foreign country where scantily dressed women offered to buy me drinks, take me for romantic walks on the beach, watch the sunset and finally accompany me back to a room to have wild orgasmic sex on a hammock. It never really appealed to me, for one, and I couldn't afford it anyway.

Besides, I'd probably throw my back out on the hammock and end up in some third world hospital. To add insult to injury, I'd also leave with something worse than I'd gone in there with.

Aside from the one perk of maintaining my health, summer vacations tended to give me too much time to think about my life. Reality could be such a stupid place, and mine was rapidly closing in. It started after I closed the van door, and we headed for home.

It wasn't the most pleasant journey in the world, mostly because it was time to start thinking about what I would do for a summer job. I really did have to think about it because I was asked about it ten minutes into the trip. Some people I knew were going off to work on boats in Alaska, others to Cedar Point or their parents' companies, and still others abroad to foreign countries to help sooth the woes of those worlds. The woes of my world began with working at Kay-Mart, an experience in itself. Working for that company period is actually a bit of a joke.

Let me say something about the Kay-Mart philosophy. Forget all the commercials on TV with happy shoppers going down well-stocked aisles talking to cream-of-the-crop professional assistants. Actually, the workers are called *asso-ciates*. Notice the word *ass* hidden at the beginning, which pretty much sums up what corporate thinks of their employees.

Furthermore, for a while, the commercials boasted that associates were being retrained. It never happened! There was never any retraining, and not much general training to speak of, since they would never pay for it.

Dustin Hoffman said it best about a similar company in *Rainman*: "K-Mart sucks."

❀ ❀ ❀

Despite the bleak beginning, the summer of 1989 was an eventful one. I'd really hoped to get a second job, one that was five days a week in the morning and paid a hell of a lot more than what I was currently getting, but that wasn't to be. There was just too much going on.

A friend of mine, Jeremy, was hit by a car while riding his bike across an intersection. The woman driving said the sun was in her eyes and she never saw him. Apparently, she must have missed the red light, too. I visited Jeremy in the hospital once, but it was too depressing to see him hooked up to so many machines, conscious yet unable to recognize who I was. It scared the hell out of me.

It didn't help that I hated hospitals. For some reason, they reminded me of the way some guys talk about how women with fake breasts feel to the touch. They say there's something ominous and sterile about them, a real strange combination.

Jeremy once told me a story about how he used to think that women had their boobs filled with helium, and that was why some of them were so large. Where the hell people got these ideas about sex and the opposite gender is beyond me.

With the exception of a health course, I never had sex education classes when I was in high school. Once in grade school—sixth grade, maybe— we had a slide show presentation that didn't tell us any more than we already knew, which was very little.

"Your bodies are changing." Well, no kidding! Tell me how. Show me some Polaroids. Let's see some people involved in one of those Kodak moments. How about letting us in on some of what we can expect to be participating in later on in life.

No such luck.

Instead of naughty little revealing shots of nudity and sex, we had a slide show and the only form of legal pornography available in the public school system: *National Geographic*. If Jeremy thought some of the women he saw had large breasts, he never bothered with this magazine. When not reading the standard Hardy Boys mysteries, the guys' noses were all buried in *National Geographic*. Doesn't that paint a pretty picture for sexual awareness in the 70s and early 80s? It's a twisted way to grow up thinking that when a woman is naked she's also holding a blowgun.

I sincerely doubt that I made a conscious decision to go the gay route because of that, however. If nothing else, it made me respect women all the more because they were just as capable of beating someone's ass as any man I'd ever seen.

Despite all the material presented to us, we still didn't know what sex was. Even after the experimentation I did with some of my friends, I never really knew if I was doing things the right way or not.

My father sat me down one night for "the talk" with "the books." I think this was in fourth grade. Anyway, I knew what felt good when I was naked with another person—a guy at least—but I had no idea they had instruction manuals for it.

If I recall correctly, one of the books was titled *Where Did I Come From?* Let me just say that it told me way more than I ever wanted to know about my mother. There seemed to be a section missing, though, one about sex between two guys. Since Dad didn't mention it to me, I guessed sex was just supposed to be the male/female thing—or had I discovered something the authors hadn't?

Dad got through that night pretty much unscathed, though I don't know if he expected to encounter problems or questions he couldn't handle. Thinking back to the grading system they had back then in school, I would have given him an

O for *outstanding*.

Naturally, I did have a question for my father, and it related to that white stuff the book called "sperm." I'd yet to see anything like that come out of me, and I wondered what it looked like so I would know in the future when it did. Despite his assurances that I would know when the time came, I demanded a description. I guess I can be sadistic that way.

Then too, so can he. I avoided Oreo cookies and tapioca pudding for months after that.

※ ※ ※

Two really cool things did eventually happen to me that summer. First, I got a car, or rather, a battle tank. My first car was an old maroon '78 Chevy Malibu. Suffice to state that this thing would have given Stephen King's Christine nightmares, to say nothing of what it must have contributed to the pollution hanging over the suburbs of Detroit. Mom and Dad didn't need to buy me a beeper to know where I was. All they had to do was look outside with a pair of binoculars and scan the distance for the smoke signals I was sending them compliments of the oil I was burning.

From the moment the damn thing died, I vowed I would never get such an old, ugly car again. No way! I wanted style, something I could show off, something I could drive without other motorists cursing me because they couldn't breathe driving behind me.

Mom, Dad, and I drove around for a couple of weeks and looked at cars, but they thought I was being too picky or too much of a smartass. Maybe I did set my sights a little high, but I felt they were setting theirs a little low. I wanted something that would take people's breath away. They wanted something affordable that wouldn't take our combined savings away.

The battle was joined for two weeks. At the end of that time, my input was deemed no longer necessary. There was a car for sale in a Bob Evans Restaurant parking lot that my parents looked over and thought was worth checking into. My part in this adventure was to write down all vital information about the vehicle, including the name and number of the person selling it and also where we saw it. I didn't especially care for the car but decided to take another route other than verbal to display my feelings on the matter.

It was embarked on shortly after we got home when Mom called the seller up.

"Hello, I'm calling regarding the car you have for sale up at Robert Evans' parking lot. No, Robert Evans. Oh, wait a second. My son wrote the information down. It should read 'Bob Evans.' Yes, I'm sorry. He's a little strange that way. Yes, I know. Children. What? Oh, no, he just turned nineteen, not nine. It surprises us, too.

"Now, I do have the information written down, and I would just like to make sure it's accurate. Would that be okay? Great. So, you have an eighteen-seventy-seven...It's nineteen-seventy-seven? He was trying to write quickly, and it probably just looked like an eight to me instead of a nine. Okay, a nineteen-seventy-seven queer brown dookie-mobile?' Yes, I agree the description does sound a bit unusual. It's dark brown? And a Turismo? I'm writing this down. Now, does it have heat and air? Heat, no air. Wait a moment, my son has a question. You want to know how you're supposed to breathe in a car with no air? I am not asking that! Sorry, it wasn't relevant. I do see there are some extras here. There's a 'working radio?' Good. 'Cassette deck?' Excellent. And the 'two rotting corpses in the trunk?'

"You know what? Can I call you right back? Thank you."

Mom just didn't see the humor in the approach I was taking to tell them I wasn't overly thrilled with their find. She immediately called a conference with her co-war chief and declared that I was to be eliminated from the selection process. On one hand, maybe I lost that war, but on the other, I didn't get that car.

I was working in the Patio department of Kay-Mart about a week later when a car pulled up to the loading area. Mom was waving to me from the window.

"Oh, Holy Mary, Mother of God," I mumbled while smiling at the same time and waving back.

It was large, old, affordable, maroon and soon to be mine.

Despite how I make the 1979 Ford LTD sound, it was a solid choice, and I did go up a year from the Malibu. Mom and Dad just wanted me to be protected in case I ever got into an accident, and a tank like an LTD was a pretty strong guarantee that I had a good chance of surviving.

It wasn't like those little aluminum foil cars that crunch like a beer can during a simple fender-bender. It had heat and air, but no radio. I was told that would be taken care of at Christmas, though, when I could go and pick one out as my gift. There was quite a bit of room in the trunk and backseat, which was going to be nice when transporting all my crap back up to school in the fall.

"It's a nice car," one of the sixteen-year-old stockboys who happened to be out there teased.

"Piss off." I really wasn't ready to have to defend it to my friends, let alone some little shit who would never attain any position above stockboy. "A Matchbox car would look nice to someone like you."

"At least I'm in *high school* and working here, not college," he called back out over his shoulder while walking away.

"Oh, yeah? Great future for you, too! You'll be the only person I know going through life pushing doors marked pull."

The little SOB did have a point. He was only in high school, and ignorance wasn't so much bliss for kids his age as it was a way of life. It had only been in the last six months that I'd become seriously interested in a career, but even so it was a bit vague. What kind of life could a writer have? What was it, exactly, that I wanted to write? Each decision I made in life only brought up more questions. That was hardly fair.

Despite all the possibilities I might one day have going for me, if I ever bothered to narrow down my interests, I felt as if something was missing. No, perhaps not something, but some*one*. What good was life if one couldn't share it with another? I saw people walking around campus with a significant other while I walked alone. I missed that closeness, and began to resent others for having what I was missing. Why should they be happy when I wasn't?

A friend of mine told me once to look at any situation that seemed unhappy to me in an optimistic way—as a glass that was half-full as opposed to half-empty, that things would get better. All I wondered was who the son of a bitch was who drank out of my glass without my noticing!

My friend said I missed the point.

Why couldn't people see that I was in need of some human compassion, and that I was as starved for love as the next person? Was I that good at hiding my feelings, or was I expressing them to the wrong people? I didn't know how to relate to others, and it seemed they were in no hurry to find a way to relate to me, so what the hell was I supposed to do? I was obviously trying to relate to people in terms they didn't understand and needed to find some common ground. I could do that, couldn't I?

❋ ❋ ❋

I needed a vacation from my vacation. The car was a pleasant addition to my life, but I doubted it would take me far enough away from work or reality. Calgon, take me away...

Oh, fuck Calgon! How far away was far enough, anyway? Far enough for me would be on some desert island where other people weren't.

But then, if I was alone, I'd never have sex, and that would mean I'd never achieve the next stage of enlightenment. Could sharing an orgasm really be that powerful? I wondered if it would be as life-changing as when I saw my first picture of Samantha Fox in the buff. Was it absolutely necessary for people to have sex to understand one another or, at least, understand themselves? If I had sex once, would everything I was missing in

28

life suddenly come into focus? Was that what the destruction of childhood innocence really was?

I wanted to have sex, just not with anyone I knew.

A relationship wouldn't be such a bad thing to have, either, before having sex. But who would I have this relationship with? Good question, and there wasn't a forthcoming answer. It had to be some woman I'd never laid eyes on yet.

I certainly didn't want to have sex or a relationship with any *guy* I knew. That wasn't even a consideration, especially since the only gay men I ever heard described—in jokes—were ugly, in their thirties and forties and had long hair, mustaches and tattoos. I didn't look like they did, I didn't talk with a major lisp and I sure as hell wasn't attracted to anyone with those qualities. If I ever did start to fall under the influence of some person like that, I hoped one of my friends would have the decency to shoot me and put me out of my misery before word ever got out.

Was I even ready for a relationship? Could I handle one maturely and sincerely enough? Did I even deserve one? It wasn't like I would have opportunities to cheat on a girlfriend, as women weren't exactly beating down my door; and it wasn't like sex had ever been an issue with me, as far as me wanting it more than she did. In many ways, maybe I was a nice guy after all.

On the other hand, nice guys were said to finish last, and I was certainly living *that* cliché.

Todd would have told me to just rent a porno film and work my frustrations out that way. That really wasn't my style, but I did go to the video store. While there, I ran into one of the jerks I graduated high school with. I had *Spacehunter— Adventures In The Forbidden Zone* in my hand, and he had *Big Busty Women Vol. 2.* It made me wonder which one of us was going to have a better time watching our movie. I'd seen *Spacehunter* about fifteen times, but he'd probably seen *Big Busty Women Vol. 1* and then moved on to the sequel.

I wondered if that made him more in touch with reality and sexuality because he could move on to T&A while I was still stuck in SF.

The whole pornography issue is a funny thing with people. In straight guys' minds, or at least the ones I knew, a woman and a man, two women and a man, one woman and two men or just two women having sex is perfectly acceptable. However, two guys having sex on camera is completely deviant. Two women making out and/or having sex with each other at a private bachelor party is hot and a real turn-on. Yet, two guys having sex in the privacy of their own home is a crime, and two guys showing any kind of public display of affection could get them a street justice death penalty. Gee, that's not the least bit hypocritical.

Yet another thought to keep to myself.

A great many thoughts and emotions were building up inside me. One moment I was dissing gays in my mind and in another I was actually defending them. By dissing them, I was in touch with the male part of me that popular society wanted to emphasize. Since popular society never held much regard for me, I refused to hold much regard for it.

This, in turn, allowed me to explore other areas

of deep thought. If there is or ever could be such a thing as a bottomless cup of coffee. Why people called it rush hour when nothing moved. Just how many licks does it take to get to the center of a Tootsie Roll Pop. Women still counted as a mystery, and probably would in any century. They were still a mystery to me, at least.

What did they think about me? That I was a geek? A few maybe thought I was a gay geek. Why did they think I was...that way? That really pissed me off! Just because I didn't go out every weekend and pick up some woman to have sex with or hit on someone at work during the week and use her to warm up for the weekend, suddenly I'm gay? I don't think so.

I was trying to be a nice guy and do things with the best of intentions, but something was inevitably going wrong.

Everything, however, was about to change.

⁂

I'm quite sure whoever coined the phrase "all things happen for a reason" was brutally murdered in cold blood by someone he or she told that to. Religious crusades, world wars, famine, poverty, disease, hate crimes, Superman IV—why? I never understood the reasons behind things like those.

My mother was, unfortunately, one of the followers of this phrase; she couldn't answer any of my questions, but she found wisdom in it, nonetheless. Most of the time I wanted to throttle her when she brought it up.

There were, however, rare instances when something happened that didn't seem particularly important at the time but that led to something else, which led to something else, and so on. In the end, something good happened.

"Andy!" Mom's voice broke me out of a stupor. "Come let the dog out!"

I was in my room with the door closed, bored out of my mind and doing absolutely nothing about it. At least boredom was *something*, and it beat letting the dog out. Furthermore, my room was on the far side of the house, and it sounded like Mom was in the kitchen. The back door was about five feet from her and a good forty feet from me, so naturally it made sense for me to have to go and do it. What was she doing that she couldn't open a screen door and let the arrogant furry bitch out?

"Andy, now!"

I sighed, stretched, opened my door and started down the hall. On the way to the kitchen, I passed the living room and Dad sitting in his recliner. That put him about twenty feet from the back door to my forty. He was twice as close and doing exactly the same thing I was doing. This couldn't be the reason my parents had me.

I was never good for lawn care and vehicle maintenance, but I'd be damned if I was going to be the dog's servant!

Actually, I wasn't good at a great many things I didn't like. Watering the flowers? Forget it. I put the spray on hard enough to kill the damn things because I wanted to get it done faster. Any parent in their right mind would have caught on after the first few incidents, but not mine. No, they continued to torture me with that task and yell when the ground and flowers looked as though they'd been through an asteroid storm.

"Andy!"

Dad flashed me a wicked grin before I continued on into the kitchen.

Mom was cutting something up in the sink while Kira, our Siberian husky, barked from the back door. She probably didn't even have to go out. The bitch played games like that. She would see that one of us was doing something then get it in her head she wanted to do something, too. At that point, we would have to stop what we were doing so she could do what she wanted. The back door game was one of her primary sources of canine amusement. As soon as she got outside and saw that we had gone back upstairs to do whatever it was she had interrupted us from doing in the first place, she would bang against the door to be let back in.

This, however, made it difficult to discern when she *really* had to go out or whether we could safely ignore her.

"I'm here, I'm here. Life goes on. Life continues. The dog will feel the sunlight on her hairy body." I opened the door and let her out.

"Where have you been? I've been calling you for ten minutes." Mom wasn't in a good mood, and I didn't think I was about to help it much.

"I counted three minutes, and I'm sorry." I spoke in a tone of mock submissiveness. "I was far away in my room working, not right at the kitchen sink or in the next room sitting on a recliner. I'll hasten to comply much faster next time."

She glared at me.

"Is there anything else I can do for you? Move the house a little to the left?"

The look on her face was the only response I was

going to get. It was all I really needed.

"I'll go outside and start pushing."

The buzzing and whirring of an electric weed whipper caught my attention. Mable!

Mable was a sixty-five-year-old divorced lady from England who lived next door. The woman had a heart of gold, but as she said about herself quite frequently, the "lights are on but nobody's home." It was a good thing she had a sense of humor because I often played practical jokes on her when I wasn't driving her to the movie theatre to watch one of our "spooky movies" or to the mall so she could get a coffee at Kresge's. Maybe she didn't always understand all the movies we watched or the pranks I played on her, but she never held anything against me and we always had fun.

One thing was for sure—I needed some fun right about now.

🌿 🌿 🌿

I grabbed the portable phone before I left the house and entered in Mable's number. Just as it was about to connect, I turned it off. Oh, this was going to be devious!

I walked out the back door and opened the gate to our driveway, careful that Kira didn't try and make a break for it. If I had to stay at home all these years, there was no way in hell she was getting out. She eyed me for a moment, but didn't bark.

It's said that a dog will take after its owners. Kira was no exception, and she tended to take after me in the area of mischief. I think she knew what I was up to, so she wasn't going to express her dismay just yet. It was better to wait and see what happened.

34

There was a hedgerow between our house and Mable's, with just enough room between the shrubs for me to slip through. She was out by the fence at the far end of the yard with her back to me. Several extension cords ran from the inside of the house, out the back door and along the ground to where she was now picking up the weeds she'd just cut. As she was putting them into a garbage bag, I ran over to the nearest cord and unplugged it but left it close enough to the other one that she would think it had just slipped out. No harm done.

I moved back behind the bushes and ducked below them for cover. She might not be able to see me, but I could see her.

Mable reached down for the weed whipper a moment later and pressed the button to start the motor. Nothing happened. She tried it a few times more to make sure she wasn't doing something wrong and then set it back down.

She looked a bit confused but finally decided to investigate. Starting at her end, she methodically worked her way up the line until she found the break in the cords near me. Her brow was furrowed, and she mumbled something as she plugged the cords back together and tested them to make sure they stayed firm.

I ran out and pulled them apart again as she was on her way back down to the end of the yard then watched as she picked up the machine.

"Shit!" I heard the agitation in her voice as plain as in my mother's. Yep, she was getting worked up pretty quickly, and I watched as she again set the machine down on the ground—a little harder than the last time. She found the two cords barely sepa-

35

rated and plugged them back together.

I again ran out and unplugged them before she got to the end of the yard. She didn't bother setting the machine down nicely this time. She tossed it as if it was somehow the tool's fault for not having any power.

"Son of a bitch. Damn cords..." She stared, really *stared*, at the two ends that refused to stay together.

After testing to make sure there was enough slack in the line and that they weren't stretched, she decided on a different course of action. She stomped into the house, and I waited for several minutes for her to return. She did, finally, only with reinforcements.

She carefully wrapped electrical tape around the two uncooperative ends then made several attempts to see if they would pull apart when she tugged on the line. They stayed together perfectly.

It was a close call, but I managed to unwrap the cords just enough, pull them apart and then rewrap them before she got to the end of the yard. When she picked up the machine, all set to work whipping away, and nothing happened, it wasn't pretty. Mable didn't swear very often, but when she got started, she was like a sailor with Tourette syndrome.

"Goddamn fucking cords! Son of a bitch! I'll glue those little fucking bastards together! Shit!"

I had to fight like hell to not laugh out loud. God, I had to be a sick kid having this much fun at the expense of a sweet elderly woman. Damn if I didn't get a kick out of it, though.

Mable practically flew up to the ends of the cords

and unwrapped the tape and scratched her head in wonder as to how in the hell they came apart. I figured she'd suffered enough, so I stood up and pretended I'd just come from the house.

"Hey, Mable," I greeted her, all smiles. "You having some trouble?"

"These fu—damn cords won't stay together." She tried to watch her language around me. "Can't get a damn thing done back there!"

"Did you try taping them together?" If there was anything sicker than what I had already done, it was the fact I could keep a straight face and look completely innocent when I had to.

She held up the cords with the tape around them.

"And they still got loose?"

"Yeah, but I don't know how." She was thoroughly frustrated. "I wrapped the shit out of them."

"Sounds to me like someone's playing games with you," I teased and put my hands on my hips.

"Could be, could be..."

It suddenly dawned on her that I was smiling a little too widely and acting just a little too nonchalant about the whole matter. Plus, I'd practically just told her I'd done it.

Her face dropped with realization. "You little asshole!"

Well, there went the language.

"I'm sure they'll stay together now." I winked at her, and she shook her head. While she was debating what to say next, I moved my left hand from my hip to my back pocket and turned the portable phone on. A moment later, I hit the redial.

"I'm sure they will, too."

37

"Mable, your phone is ringing."

"Oh!" She perked up and made a mad dash for her back door. Mable didn't get too many phone calls since she got divorced. Most of the time, it was either one of her three kids—two of them mainly when they needed money, the third was okay—her employer, me or a friend. Mable just loved company and talking, so she always ran when the phone rang.

I moved to a position where I could see her through the back door, and just as she was about to pick the receiver up, I turned the phone off. She came back outside a few seconds later, a disappointed look on her face.

"Who was it?" I asked innocently.

"I got there too late. They hung up." She looked completely dejected.

God, I suddenly felt sorry for her. The poor woman was only trying to get some yardwork done, and I'd managed to put a damper on that. The only thing I could think to do to make it up to her was annoy her so thoroughly with something else that she'd completely forget the entire weed whipper incident.

I was nothing if not logical, and since I'd already started taking her mind off things with the phone, I felt obligated to continue on with it.

"I'm sure whoever it was will call you back," I reassured her. "You're generally home at this time of night, so they probably figured you were on the toilet or in the shower." I pressed the redial button.

"You think so?" Mable considered my logic.

"Absolutely."

The phone could be heard ringing again.

"See? There you go."

Mable ran for the door, and I once more hung up just as she was about to grab the receiver.

"*Shit!*"

She waited a few seconds more before coming outside, probably thinking that maybe they would call back one last time. When it didn't ring again, she returned, and she brought a broom out with her.

This just wasn't her night, and I would have one hell of a story to tell at the dinner table.

"They hung up again?" I asked.

"I wish I knew who it was." She shook her head. "I'd like to kick their ass for making me run like that!"

"I hear ya," I commiserated. "If somebody did that to me, I'd want to hurt them, too."

Her phone began to ring, only this time it wasn't me. How the hell did I get her to run once more without giving myself away?

"Uh, Mable? I think you better go answer that."

"Fuck it! I've had it with answering those hang-up calls. It's probably just some prick pranking me."

"No, I really think you should answer this one." I reluctantly continued, "It's for real."

I couldn't help but give it away at this point because it could have been an important call.

"What do you mean 'It's for real'?" Mable was definitely suspicious.

"I'll see you later." I turned around, completely forgetting I had the phone in my back pocket. There was just this sudden feeling that I should be getting along home that took hold of me.

Mable didn't miss the phone in my back pocket. It took a moment for it to register, but then she realized what I'd done to her.

"You little asshole!" She swung the broom at my ass and just barely missed. "I can't wait for you to go to California so I'll have some peace and quiet!"

I had to think of something quick to get her mind off beating the hell out of me.

"Your phone is still ringing!" I ran for my yard.

"Oooh!" She turned quickly and made one last mad dash inside. I waited just long enough to see if she made it. "Son-of-a-bitch!"

Apparently, she didn't.

"Things happen for a reason," I muttered and wondered what was up with this California thing.

3

I mentioned some time back that there were two important events that took place during the summer before my sophomore year of college. The first was getting the car. The second occurred after Mable let that hint slip in her rage. If it hadn't been for her, I never would have known I was under close observation to determine if I was capable of behaving well enough to accompany my grandmother to California for six days for her brother's fiftieth wedding anniversary.

Apparently, Grandma's alcoholic gentleman friend Roberto disliked traveling anywhere far beyond his own yard and absolutely refused to go to "the Big C" with her. After a month of trying to convince him and getting nowhere, she became determined that someone else would get the pleasure of being her escort. Roberto would just have to drink by himself for awhile.

None of this bothered me in the least. I couldn't care less who I was going with as long as I got to go. Here was that much-needed vacation I had been searching for, and I think it was safe to say that

California was far enough away. It was almost too good to be true!

Basking in the hot California sun and surrounded by voluptuous babes rubbing suntan lotion all over my body was a fantasy that every straight man dared to dream. What I didn't have in physique to thrill them I would make up for in character. I'd always wanted an opportunity to find love and had secretly been praying for it, along with asking to pass my exams, and He'd finally answered. All those times people warned about being careful what one asked for—how could this possibly go wrong?

❦ ❦ ❦

Work gave me the time off I needed. I knew that wouldn't be a problem since asses—associates have such a high turnover rate. The day of departure finally arrived, and Grandma and I were driven to the airport in the early afternoon. I loved how the time worked. We would take off at one p.m. in Michigan and arrive about two or two-thirty p.m. in California. This meant we only lost about an hour.

One of Grandma's other brothers and his wife were going to pick us up, and we would all drive directly to the party. I have to say I wasn't really looking forward to this anniversary thing. I just wanted to be dropped off at the beach and picked up afterwards.

Grandma and I had never had the pleasure of traveling with each other before. Even when I was younger, I rarely spent a night at her place, and I understood why. Her first husband was a violent alcoholic who used to beat her and burn her clothes in the incinerator. Her second husband was also an abusive alcoholic, but more of a verbal one. It made spending time with her very difficult, but it wasn't like we didn't have a bond. After all, she gave me some really cool Christmas and birthday gifts and money for graduation and other holidays or festivities. I just wanted something on a more emotional level, with mutual trust and respect, which she was either unable or unwilling to work on with me.

Still, it didn't mean we couldn't have fun. For instance, Grandma took the lead and headed for the bar the moment we checked our luggage in.

"Let's get a drink." She spoke with some urgency.

That was all fine and dandy for her, but I wasn't of legal drinking age yet. While that never bothered or stopped me up at school, I couldn't exactly get away with it in public. Then, too, it occurred to me that people were supposed to do things on vacation they didn't normally do when they were at home.

Why was she drinking, then? Maybe the one drink would sooth Grandma's nerves, just on the off-chance she also didn't like flying.

After the third drink, however, I was getting the impression Grandma was only going to be happy after she *deadened* her nerves as opposed to merely soothing them. I, on the other hand, was on a caffeine high.

By the time the plane was ready to taxi down the runway, Grandma had this glazed look in her eyes and a half-cockeyed smile on her face. The only real tip-off that she was pleasantly on her way to a drunken stupor was the little bit of drool slowly starting to drip from the corner of her mouth. Well, there was also the open little bottles—vodka in her left hand and peach schnapps in the right.

For as much she liked to drink, she still looked wonderful on the outside. I only hoped I had her genetic heritage in my liver.

It never ceases to amaze me how much taking off in an airplane feels as close to an orgasm as one can get without actually having one. I'm not embarrassed about it because it happens to be a shared experience. Some people like to be drunk when it happens, others have panic attacks and yet others just sit back and enjoy the ride. All in all, I guess it's very much like having sex, though slightly more expensive unless you're paying for a high-priced hooker. I've gotten the same thrill off a Ferris wheel at a carnival before and that was only seventy-five cents.

I could never understand why comedians always tell stories about how horrible their flights to wherever they were going were. At least they got to travel first class! I never did yet. I also never got to sit next to some overweight person who spilled over into my seat, never sat behind someone who insisted on remaining reclined the entire trip and never sat in front of some little brat who kicked my seat. I have, however, been gypped out of my bag of peanuts and been overlooked by the stewardess serving a meal.

Before when I've flown, I've been alone. Not this time. No, I was with Mary Poppins and her *other* traveling companion, Jack Daniels. At least she was quiet for the trip and somewhat lucid for the landing.

We had barely stepped into the terminal when our welcoming party shouted out to us, "Hey,

Hotdog!"

"Oh, shit," I mumbled. It was my Great-uncle Chester and his wife Virginia. This really was going to be an interesting ride to Covina.

Uncle Chester always called Grandma "Hotdog" and the other members of the family by some other little pet name; but for some reason, he always had trouble remembering mine—my real name, that is. He also had a reputation for being a bigger pain-in-the-ass than I could ever aspire to be. I liked him well enough when he wasn't talking to me and enjoyed his jokes when I wasn't the butt of them, but I was going to be sharing closer quarters with him than I ever had before.

His wife was fairly quiet, which was a nice contrast to her husband. Nobody really knew too much about her, though. Maybe I'd get an opportunity to start a conversation with her during the trip.

Starting a conversation with Uncle Chester was never a problem. He reminded me of one those drips a faucet sometimes developed, the kind you can never turn off.

"Chester!"

Grandma set her bag down in front of me and ran over to him. Since I was blocking all the people still trying to exit the plane, I took it that I was to be her baggage boy for the moment instead of her grandson. I kept my temper in check and watched as she gave Uncle Chester a huge, tight hug and then a kiss. I wondered how he could stay standing and not get dizzy after smelling her breath. It still had to be at least 40-proof.

Shortly after, Grandma greeted Aunt Virginia

and gave her a quick peck on the cheek and a soft hug, hardly the greeting her brother had received. Aunt Virginia was apparently very fragile and had to be handled with care, as it appeared too-rapid inhalation and exhalation of air from her lungs might damage her irreparably.

The three of them talked for a few minutes while I stood by and waited for them to finish. Grandma finally started looking around, presumably for her bag, and then saw me with it. It seemed for a moment she was going to ask me why I had her luggage and then remembered I was a relative who had just happened to fly out with her. Recognition is such a beautiful thing in life.

"Chester, Virginia, you remember my..." Grandma looked confused for a moment, as if still trying to place me. "This is Marie and Donald's son."

"Andy." I extended my hand to Uncle Chester. "The grandson."

"Well!" Uncle Chester snatched me up, almost off the ground, and gave me the same kind of hug Grandma had given him. "Of course you are!"

"Whoa." I nearly gagged, and he set me down. "It's Miller time." I now understood why he didn't get dizzy after smelling Grandma's breath. They were two peas that belonged together in the same pod. I couldn't wait to meet the rest of the family, assuming they were allowed out of the Betty Ford Clinic for the anniversary, that is.

"That's a great idea, Adam!" Uncle Chester looked at me with approval in his eyes. "Hotdog, he's family, all right. We've got a few minutes to kill, so why don't we go hit the airport bar for a drink and you can tell me how your flight was."

"We have to get our lug—" Grandma only managed to get that out before she was cut off.

"Oh, nonsense!" Uncle Chester put one arm around her and the other around his wife. "The kid can get all the bags then find us at the bar. He has to earn his keep somehow." He turned them around then looked at me over his shoulder and winked. "Go bust your hump, Alex. I'll buy you a water afterwards."

I was ready to go bust something, all right, and it wasn't my hump! What the hell was up with Grandma, anyway? She was going to tell Uncle Chester about the trip? She probably couldn't even *remember* the damn trip! I didn't get a chance to say hello to Aunt Virginia, either. The poor woman was going to be so confused by the time I had another opportunity she'd never be able to remember my name, either. Grandma was off the plane for five minutes and the only thing she could remember was that I happened to be "Marie and Donald's child." Isn't that lovely?

I just hoped to God that the fact he was only going to buy me a glass of water didn't mean I'd suddenly become the designated driver.

It took about twenty minutes before the luggage started filtering out along the conveyor. As I should have expected, considering how the trip had gone so far, ours were almost the last to come out. To make matters worse, while I only brought one large suitcase, Grandma had two. I thought at first maybe she had just brought the second one to pack whatever she decided to bring back as gifts for the rest of the family. Nope. It was full, and there weren't rollers on the bottom of it. I would have thought that, with the amount of money she spent on spirits, she could afford a newer suitcase with rollers.

Old people are so damn stuck on the philosophy "If it works..." It doesn't work! I know. I had to carry her two while dragging my own behind me. By the time I found the others, I was out of breath, out of strength and needing that fucking water!

"We were wondering where you were." Uncle Chester looked at his watch. "Took your time, eh? Well, you may have set us back a little bit, so I guess I'll just have to try and make up for it on the freeway. Come on, Hotdog!"

The three of them stood up and exited the bar. The only thing I could do was stand there. It seemed the peaceful thing to do, and it beat screaming or throwing things. Just blessed nothingness...

Grandma peeked her head around the corner a moment later. Did she offer to help me with her suitcases? No. Did she offer her brother's help with her suitcases? No. She gave me a dirty look and snapped her fingers to get me to follow. The only reason I picked everything up again and started after them was so I could find a very tall overpass on the way to the car and chuck her cases over the side.

Between her continued dirty looks, finger-snaps, and Uncle Chester's never-ceasing complaints about how slow I was and that I could be "outrun by any ninety-year-old in a wheelchair," it was a damn good thing there *wasn't* an overpass.

We finally arrived at the car.

"Well, Hotdog, what do you think?" Uncle

Chester gestured grandly with his hand at the chariot that awaited us.

"An economy car," I spoke up, "and a small one at that. How quaint." Where the hell we were going to fit everything into this vehicle was beyond me. Then again, perhaps he would just suggest tying me to the roof or bumper. After all, it seemed I was expendable.

"Virginia thought we should bring the minivan," Uncle Chester admitted, "but I didn't really see the point. Why spend the extra money using up all that gas when we can get better mileage out of this?" He opened up a trunk that actually made the rest of the vehicle look much larger. There was no way we could fit three suitcases in it. "Know what I mean?"

"Absolutely," I agreed with him and shook my head. "Without a doubt." I mumbled the next part as I started squeezing two of the suitcases into the small confined area. "Why go somewhere comfortably when you can travel in something the size of a can of Spam?"

The last case just wasn't going to fit. What we were going to do with it was a mystery.

"Uncle Chester?"

All three of them came over and looked at me with disapproval.

"This isn't going to work."

"That's because ya don't know what you're doing!" He looked in the trunk and shook his head. "Why don't you go make yourself useless and I'll fix it."

Why not? I've made it a habit in life to make myself useless when I wasn't needed, so I let him deal with it. If Roberto had come with Grandma, he'd either be having the time of his life or he'd be thinking about throttling Uncle Chester, too. At least now I understood why nobody else wanted to come here with Grandma—I was the family's sacrificial goat.

The whole situation made me start to wonder if my life had really been as difficult as I'd thought before I left home. If I'd wanted to be treated like a Kay-Mart employee, I could have stayed there. On the other hand, *this was California*, home of some of the most sexually attractive and sexually hungry women on the face of the planet! Even I couldn't possibly strike out here, especially since there was a rumor there were women in this state who couldn't find enough men to give them what they desired, so they turned to various kinds of fruit for pleasure. I would be just one more virgin cast out onto a sea of women waiting to engulf me.

"I think we have it worked out." Grandma spoke up from in back and walked around to the front with Aunt Virginia. "We'll sit in back," she told her, "and let...Marie and Donald's son sit in front. There's a little more room up there, and we shouldn't be too cramped in back."

Other than the fact she still couldn't remember my name, I thought it was the first sensible thing she'd said yet. I was six feet tall, and there was no way on God's earth I could have managed to fit in the backseat of that dinky little economy car. Why they called it an economy car was no great mystery. It probably got the same kind of mileage as all the other cars, only with half the room.

Economy car or not, I was glad Grandma was thinking of me and how squished I would be if I had to ride in the back. It just wouldn't have been pretty.

"And I shall graciously accept the front." I winked at the two women, but they merely glared at me. It was as if I'd said something entirely inappropriate. Since when was taking the front seat such an offense? Should I be complaining? Would that make them happier? Old people could be funny that way.

"Of course you're taking the front!" Uncle Chester ushered me inside the car after Grandma climbed into the backseat. "You didn't expect any of the ladies to drive with this on their lap, did you?"

He forced my suitcase through the door and succeeded in scraping my jaw and then setting it to rest with one corner on my groin. All I could do was groan as I desperately tried to rearrange it in a better position.

"Well, Axel..." Uncle Chester patted me on the shoulder. "...that will teach you to pack a little lighter next time."

He shut the door, but one of the corners of the suitcase was sticking out a little and it didn't close tight. Instead of helping me rearrange things a bit, he opened it then swung it shut harder and looked satisfied when it stayed.

❦ ❦ ❦

The seventy minutes to Covina was a long, painful and hot experience. It was long because Uncle Chester only drove fifty-five miles an hour, which increased our travel time from the original theoretical seventy minutes to almost two hours. His idea of making up for the time we had lost at the airport apparently meant going the speed limit, as it wasn't such a good idea to push an economy car up to the speeds that all the yuppies drove. He informed us that speeds fifty-five and above were the reasons they had to get their cars replaced so often, and he hated contributing to an already corrupt capitalist system.

The ride was painful because I was never able to reposition my suitcase. All I could do was lift it up off *that* area as best I could and pray he didn't hit too many bumps, which of course he managed to do with uncanny precision.

Making things even worse was that Uncle Chester didn't have a clue how to operate his air conditioner.

"Chester," Grandma said, "would you turn the air on? Virginia and I are really uncomfortable."

"It is on, Hotdog. Probably just isn't warmed up enough to send out the cool air." He gave me a sidelong look. "Amos's bag here is probably blocking the breeze. Hope that isn't too heavy for you, kid. Maybe you should start working out, put some muscles on those girly little arms of yours."

He winked at me, and I felt like poking his eye out.

"It's been warming up for thirty minutes. You have to push the A/C button down once," Grandma told him impatiently, "otherwise it just circulates the air that's already in the car and it doesn't cool—"

"I know what I'm doing, Hotdog." He frowned and gave her a dirty look in the mirror. "It's either broken or that's as cool as it gets. Economy car, you know?" His good humor returned. "Those air conditioners they have in all those other yuppie cars, why, I'll just bet every time they get used it shortens a hundred miles off the life of the car. Pretty soon, you have to go and buy another new car, and the carmakers have found even better ways to take the life out of that car in a lot shorter time. One of these years, we'll have to get a new car every time we want to go out and drive. I hope I don't live to see that day."

I hoped not, either, and it had nothing to do with having the satisfaction of proving him right or wrong. It just had to do with satisfaction.

Grandma persisted. "But if you push the button down, you'll see—"

"Hey!" Uncle Chester raised his voice. "Who's doing the driving here, missy?" He tried to reclaim his calm. "Now, the air is working just fine, so sit back and enjoy the sights."

Sights? Oh, the freeway—a sight we *never* saw back home. No, *we* just had dirt roads, and horse-drawn carriages.

Everyone in the car knew he didn't have a clue what he was talking about. It had probably never occurred to him to push the A/C button down or that it was even a button at all. How long had the two of them owned the car and never bothered using the air conditioner?

I also figured he was too stubborn to get the manual out and look to see if he was doing something wrong. Well, he was *incapable* of doing anything wrong, so why would he get the book out? It was easier to believe the car didn't work properly. Consequently, he had learned to enjoy the heat.

Being from Michigan, Grandma and I were

extremely finicky about our environment. During the winter, we both had to have heat. In the summer, it was the opposite. Her brother was only accustomed to heat year-round, so it really didn't bother him like it did us. I was uncomfortable to begin with, but the lack of cool air was making me sweat all the more. If something didn't happen soon, I was going to end up a sweaty, smelly, wrinkled heap by the time we reached the party.

I would have suggested that Uncle Chester press the button for the hell of it, but he would no more listen to me than his own sister. In fact, he would probably be even more condescending to me than her, and I really didn't want to go that route.

Grandma was apparently so uncomfortable by now she was willing to risk ignoring her brother and take a course of action that would alleviate her discomfort. Mimicking a stretch, she extended her arms and tapped lightly on the right side of my head, out of view of Uncle Chester. I gave her a dirty look in the side mirror and mouthed the word *What?* She nonchalantly raised a finger and made pushing motions with it.

I couldn't believe it! Grandma actually expected *me* to push the button since her brother wouldn't. Little did she know that I would love to do just that but was enjoying her discomfort too much to take her request seriously. Misery loved company. I was plenty miserable and so was she, so I shook my head, essentially telling her to stuff it.

She smacked my head with such a force Uncle Chester looked over at me to see what had happened. I had to think of something fast.

"Look!" I motioned with my head towards

everyone's left. "Isn't that Johnny Carson?" Three heads whipped around to catch a glimpse of the almighty, and I used what few seconds I had to give the A/C button one quick, concise jab. Contact!

The little letters were suddenly lit in blue, and I could feel the first few drafts of the freon-cooled air blowing across my skin. Uncle Chester turned back around to make sure he wasn't going off the side of the road then took another quick glance.

"Oh, you must have missed him. Probably some yuppie driving him faster than they should be going." I took a look in the mirror and saw the half-smile on Grandma's face. She knew and approved, even if she couldn't remember my name.

"Tell me, Angus." Uncle Chester attempted small talk. "What do they teach you in that school out there? Anything good?"

"I'm still getting my general core classes out of the way. You know—like history, math and chemistry—but I should be able to start courses for my major next winter." Why the sudden interest in my education? Did it raise me up a few levels in his eyes, or was he about to try and pay me back for that yuppie wisecrack?

"Well..." He shook his head. "I don't know what good knowing chemistry will do you when you start farming." He then proceeded to make little clicking noises with his tongue to emphasize his feelings on the matter.

"Farming?" I was stumped.

"You *are* from Michigan," he told me, as if pointing out to a child that the sky was blue.

"That doesn't...I mean..." Yeah? "I'm not going to be a farmer."

"What's wrong with farmers?" Uncle Chester demanded.

"There's nothing wrong with farmers." Here was where I came across as defensive.

"Then why don't you like them?" And here was where he turned the conversation around even worse than it already was.

"I never said that." I tried to find the happy place inside my mind. "I just said that I'm not going to be one. My parents didn't spend hundreds of dollars for a chemistry class so I could put Avogadro's number to use on a farm."

"Not unless you're growing Avogadros," he persisted in a sarcastic singsong tone.

"That's avo*cados*."

"You say tomato..." Uncle Chester wasn't about to back down.

"Yes, but Avogadro was a chemist and an avocado is a fruit." So was my great-uncle.

"And so are you if you believe all that stuff they tell you." Okay, apparently, we were both fruits. There's nothing quite like family to point out all of your supposed faults. "You getting a load of this, Hotdog?" He looked up into the mirror to make sure she was, indeed, "getting this" then peered back over at me. "You going to be a ditch-digger, then?"

"No."

"Got a thing against them, too, huh?" Again came the disapproving *tsk*ing noises. "Doesn't like farmers or ditch-diggers. How does your girlfriend put up with all your prejudices?"

"He doesn't have one."

Oh, *now* Grandma remembers something about me. She couldn't recall my name, but she knew I didn't have a girlfriend. If there was any justice in this world...

"You don't have a *girlfriend?*" Here we went again. "You're not one of those—"

"*No*, I'm not one of *those.*" Whatever the hell "those" actually were. God only knew, considering I was dealing with *his* mind.

"Well, I'm glad we got that out in the open." Uncle Chester actually sounded relieved. "Don't think Virginia and I haven't heard what goes on out there with those farm animals on a lonely Friday and Saturday night. We watch *Twenty/Twenty.*"

"That's udderly ridiculous," I quipped.

"Are you calling Barbara Walters a liar?" He was riled up again as quickly as he'd settled down.

"No." I tried to get him back to his happy place. "I just made a pun. I used *udder* instead of *utter*. It was a joke."

"Does this look like a face that's laughing, Anton?"

It didn't.

"No, you're right." It was pointless to even try to defend myself. "I'm sorry. I shouldn't have made light of it."

"Because those animals have rights!" He smacked the dashboard with his hand.

"Oh, my God."

☙ ☙ ☙

The four of us arrived at the party some time and many bumps later. At least, we were much cooler than we had been at the beginning. It didn't even bother me that Uncle Chester kept rubbing it in to Grandma that he was right and that it just took the air conditioner a little while to warm up. I was just relieved he wasn't picking on me anymore. Hell, I don't even think she cared. In fact, I'm pretty sure she just tuned him out for the remaining part of the journey.

That seemed to be a family trait on my grandmother's side. If something didn't agree with them, they ignored it, maybe hoping it will shut up or go away.

I got out of the car and, after Grandma emerged from the backseat, replaced my suitcase in the front. Luckily, I had worn pants that didn't wrinkle too easily so I didn't look as bad as I'd thought I was going to. I did have trouble standing up straight after having the suitcase sitting on my crotch the entire time.

The first thing I noticed was the lack of other cars parked on the street with us. I would have thought that, for a fiftieth wedding anniversary, there would have been more people. Maybe we were early.

"This doesn't look right." Grandma spoke up as she looked around. "Chester, are you sure this is the right place? I don't recognize any of the houses, and I don't see any other cars."

"Oh," he teased her, "it's just down the street this way."

Grandma and I shared a sideways look, but Aunt Virginia had already started following him so we did, too. I wondered if my poor aunt ever spoke. For that matter, I wondered if she ever had an *opportunity* to speak. Uncle Chester seemed to have enough to say for both of them. Generally speaking, he was generally speaking.

He turned around after every block we passed

and assured us we were going in the right direction. After five blocks, I could tell Grandma was getting a little nervous and was starting to doubt her brother's memory. I'd already been doubting a great deal more than that.

"Are you sure you know where you're going?" Grandma had just about had enough guessing.

"It's only another two blocks. I just didn't want to park the car too close. We'll have an easier time getting out of the subdivision if we aren't all blocked in and waiting in line. I also hate putting that beauty in with all the other cars. I'm always afraid someone will try and take off with it."

Uncle Chester laughed heartily and then lowered his voice. "Uh, Hotdog, you may want to tell Abner there to quit walking so funny. I'm sure Chad and Richard are going to be at the party." He rolled his eyes. "They've never passed up an opportunity to flaunt themselves...and I don't think he'll want to give his cousins the wrong idea, especially since he doesn't have a girlfriend. It's bad enough what they do *outside* the family, so I think if we can avoid any additional unnecessary scenes, we should try to do so."

He gave me a piteous look and turned back around.

"Chad and Richard?" I'd never heard of these cousins. Who the hell were they, and why had Uncle Chester spoken about them with such distaste? I looked at Grandma. "What is he talking about? Flaunt what?"

"Well..." She looked uncomfortable. "...some people don't always follow in the footsteps that are best for them in life. There are a few cousins you have who will be here tonight who are like that. Sometimes..." She paused. "...they choose to ignore the morals their parents, teachers and ministers have tried to instill in them and instead go down a more...sinful path."

"Oh." I sighed in relief. That was no big deal! For crying out loud..."Why didn't you just say there were going to be politicians there?"

"Um..." She and Uncle Chester exchanged worried glances. "Not politicians." Grandma let her brother and his wife get a ways ahead of us then drew me closer to her and whispered in my ear. "Homosexuals."

"In California?" Was she kidding? I'd never actually thought to wonder where they lived before, but this was a bit of a surprise. What was the attraction to this state? Something else occurred to me—if they were in California, then they could be anywhere. Alaska. Hawaii. The Virgin Islands. Cincinnati. I wondered if there were any in Michigan. Did I know any? I might not have even known about my cousins if Uncle Chester hadn't said something. Shit! That meant they could also be anyone, and I might not be able to tell the difference.

"Well, what should I do?" My face suddenly felt very warm and my palms were sweating.

"For starters..." Grandma grabbed my shoulders and forced me to stand up straight. "...quit slouching. I never understood why you had such bad posture."

"How about..." I stared up at the sky and then back down at her in a rather dramatic manner. "...because Uncle Chester smashed my testicles with my suitcase and then repeatedly hit bumps all the way here? I know you don't have testicles, but maybe you can imagine how that felt. I'll clue you in—*painful*! It was so severe in the beginning I figured I'd have to wait a few days if I'd been planning on making any babies. After the first half-hour, though, it all went numb. And you know what? It's *still* numb. Despite being a clever insult, numb nuts are not a good thing."

Grandma didn't quite know what to say. It had probably been a long time since she'd seen a pair of testicles, but I was certain she could remember what they looked like and imagine the pain involved in what I had just been through.

As far as I was concerned, this was the last straw. Her finger-snapping-while-I-walked-two-steps-behind days were over! I didn't put up with this from my parents, so I wasn't about to put up with it from her. There were bigger fish to look out for, mainly the homosexuals. They shouldn't be too difficult to spot, so all I had to do was keep my distance. I could handle this.

"Are you okay?" Grandma meekly asked me.

"Better." I attempted to sound a bit more cheery while easing a cramp from standing up straight. "Now, come on. Uncle Chester and Aunt Virginia are waiting for us."

Grandma took my arm, and we rejoined her brother and his wife. The four of us walked together up a long winding driveway lined with limos, a few Lotuses, a brand-new Grand Prix or two and some shiny new test car I'd never seen before. I took it these were the cars Uncle Chester was concerned about. It was so obvious what an eyesore they would have looked like next to his economy vehicle.

Old people *do* think the strangest thoughts.

I wondered which ones the homosexuals drove. There weren't any outlandish colors or frilly decor on any of the interiors that I could see. Maybe they'd parked a mile away and walked, like we did.

It was a mystery that wouldn't soon be solved, since I had no intention of asking about it. No, thank you! This straight boy was his own woman…or something like that. As long as I talked and thought in the most masculine of ways—specifically, having something to do with sports—my cousins shouldn't even come near me.

"Chester, Virgy, Lizzy!" a shrill female voice shouted out. "Come in! Oh, my God, you look so great!" A woman, probably in her fifties, flew out the front door and gave Uncle Chester a huge hug. She then tenderly shook Aunt Virginia's hand and looked at Grandma. "Oh, Lizzy, it's been years." She and Grandma hugged. "I'm so glad you came. Leon is going to be so thrilled that you flew in to see us!"

"I wouldn't have missed it for the world!" Grandma hugged her again, and I could see that her eyes were tearing up. It really was a sweet moment to watch, and I naturally assumed that this woman, who had more energy than anyone half her age, was undoubtedly my aunt Carma. God, I wanted to hug her, too! The spirit of the affair was really taking a hold of me.

Aunt Carma turned and looked at me a moment after they parted, and one of the most gracious expressions I think I've ever seen appeared on her face. This woman was radiating beauty and energy in a way I had never seen before. It was as if pure grace and class flowed through her instead of blood. This was where I belonged. This was my family.

Finally, at long last, she started to speak to me, and I longed to hear her welcome me to her home and invite me in to celebrate with them on this special occasion.

"You must be the hired boy."

"What?"

I had absolutely no idea what to say to that. Because I didn't have wrinkles or age lines I was suddenly the hired help? I know this woman had pictures of me somewhere that Mom had sent in Christmas cards over the years.

"No, actually, I'm Lizzy's grandson, Andy." Nothing. No spark of recognition whatsoever. "Marie and Donald's son." I spoke through clenched teeth. I might just as well have been Donny and Marie's son, since no one recognized me. No, come to think of it, that would make me inbred. Well, I could get a hell of a scholarship...

"Of course!" Aunt Carma clasped her hands together and walked over to me. "And you look so much like your mother."

"Father," I corrected.

"Whatever." She dismissed me and turned back to the others. "Come on in and get something to eat and drink. Lizzy." Aunt Carma took Grandma's hand and patted it several times. "Let's go find your brother and get a glass of champagne. You're starting to look a little sober."

Uncle Chester leaned over and whispered in my ear, "She *is* starting to look a little gloomy."

"That's *somber*, but Grandma *is* starting to look sober so I think Aunt Carma said the right thing." Did this man even own a dictionary?

"You have nooooooo idea what you're talking about, do you, Avery?"

4

The four of them disappeared into the house. I didn't follow at first because I wasn't sure if it was safe to or not. This was really starting to piss me off! I wouldn't have been the least bit surprised to walk in and see a large demon with hooves for feet, two horns, a long pointed tail and pitchfork serving hors d' oeuvres. This wasn't a vacation as much as it was a damned identity crisis.

I took a deep breath and opened the front door. The main room was mostly empty, but the kitchen just off to the left was a hustle and bustle of activity. Staff from the catering company ran in and out of the house and downstairs for more supplies, back upstairs and then back outside again, refreshing glasses and replacing empty food trays with new little delicacies. These people were definitely earning their money. I moved farther inside.

"Excuse me, sir." A waiter had come up behind me and was anxiously trying to get past where I stood blocking the doorway between the hall and kitchen. The way he'd uttered the word *sir* had me wondering if he was rushed or merely annoyed that I was in his way.

"Sorry," I apologized goodnaturedly, and stepped aside. "I didn't mean to get in the way. I was just looking around the house. It isn't very often I get out to California to see my relatives or where they live."

"Tourists." He rolled his eyes, snorted, shook his head and started past me.

"Oh, I'm a tourist." I spoke a little too loudly. "Guess that means you don't have to be polite. Why don't I just stand here and block the way again? Then, when you come back, you can just plow me right over. Hell!" I threw up my hands. "If you get up enough speed, you can knock me back to Michigan and save me the price of a return ticket...dick."

That got his attention.

"What is your problem?" He whirled around and faced me. "You obviously have one if you feel the need to call me a dick."

At first, I thought he was going to lighten up and apologize, aware of how rude he'd just been, but then he stared at me as if expecting an answer. It caught me completely off-guard.

"Do you feel that insecure in your masculinity you have to resort to name-calling?"

"Uh...well..." Hey! He'd started this. I'd been nice about moving out of his way, and he had to go and make some snide remark about me being a tourist. "Of course I'm secure! And as for my masculinity..."

Here was where I was supposed to dazzle him by

saying something brilliant, something manly, but what? What the hell did I know that was brilliant or even remotely impressive? The only thing I could remember from chemistry is that 6.02 multiplied by ten to the twenty-third power equals one mole. That left manly, and the only thing I could think of in that respect was sports, which wasn't saying much at all. Teams! Think teams. This *was* California.

"Say, how about those Miami..." Oh, shit. I hoped my face didn't mirror the stupidity and blankness of my mind. Miami wasn't in California. To make matters worse, the Miami what? It was a fish, wasn't it? "...Mammals?"

"Miami Mammals?" Now came the look that told me I had to be the biggest moron in the world. How ironic that I should actually feel that way, too.

"Porpoises?" I asked, and he shook his head in disbelief. "Well, they're not whales..." I motioned toward my back and waved my hand. "They're the things with those flipper things on the top." Maybe I should just pay more attention to sports.

"Dolphins," he said in a tone of smug triumph.

"Yeah." I wanted to throttle him. "The Dolphins."

"What about them?"

Oh, God. There had to be another point?

"If you don't know, then perhaps *your* masculinity should be in question and not mine." Momma always says "If you can't dazzle 'em with brilliance, baffle 'em with bullshit." And why not? I was the king of it, anyway.

"Well, aren't you butch?" He retorted condescendingly, and walked away.

"No, I'm Andy." I threw up my hands in defeat.

"It's not that difficult of a name to remember."

What was up with this "Butch" thing, now? Had he been talking to Uncle Chester?

The only thing I knew for sure was that I needed a drink.

I slipped outside to where everybody else was. At first glance, there looked to be about a hundred people standing or sitting around, and the backyard looked incredible! Actually, if I didn't know it was a backyard, I would have thought it to be the patio of one of the most posh restaurants I could imagine. It was at least a triple lot, and completely surrounded by trees on all three sides, effectively cutting out any view of their neighbors' yards at all. In the center was a small landscaped waterfall, surrounded by trees as well, that emptied into a tiny pond. Ice sculptures of animals and other artistic designs surrounded the pond and were probably melting into it, which cut down on the mess they would make if they'd been on a table.

On either side of the sculptures were round tables and then a head table in the middle at the far end. A large banner hung from one end of the yard to the other that read HAPPY 50TH ANNIVERSARY LEON AND CARMA!

All the food was set up on large buffet tables on the right side of the yard. There were too many people around it to get even a glimpse of what was available, but if the stuff tasted half as good as it smelled, I was in for a real treat. No grilled cheeses and French fries this day!

I looked around for a place to sit, but most of the tables were filled, and the seats that *were* empty had glasses in front of the chairs or various articles of clothing folded over them. That was probably just as well since I didn't care to be around people at the moment, not after the experiences with Uncle Chester, Aunt Carma and the waiter from Hell.

The far left side of the yard had a couple of lounge chairs set up and small tables in between them. It was deserted except for the occasional curious straggler, so that area would suit me just fine.

Grandma found me before I could safely escape and urgently pulled me aside.

"I have to talk to you." She dug her nails into my arm.

"What?" I asked through clenched teeth. "I haven't done anything yet. What could possibly be so wrong that you have to draw blood?"

"You see those men over by the far table on the right side of the waterfall?"

She motioned with her head and let up on the nails. I peered and saw two men who looked to be in their early thirties dressed in dark slacks and light-colored short-sleeve shirts. They appeared to be related, or at least brothers. They didn't look out-of-place, and I began to wonder if I was looking at the right group.

"Those are your cousins Chad and Richard." Grandma looked as though she'd bitten into a lemon. "They're the homosexuals." She started to go back towards the party then turned and pointed a finger at me. "Keep your distance."

"Go take your Ritalin." Despite my irritation with her, there wouldn't be too much of a fight from me on that issue, since I planned on keeping my distance from everybody else anyway. All I really wanted now was a drink. It didn't matter if it was Pepsi, 7-Up or a stiff shot of vodka. I just wanted to kick back and relax for a few minutes.

I noticed a heavyset man in a designer suit with long brown hair standing with a thin elderly woman with blond hair in almost a beehive-style hairdo a few feet away from me. They had been desperately trying to get the attention of one of the waiters, and he was finally coming over with a tray of glasses and bottle of champagne. I joined them to get one, too. Much to my surprise, the heavier one wasn't a man at all but another woman. I realized this when I looked at her from the front and heard her speak, though she did have an accent.

"Oy, waiter person!" She hurried the waiter over to us. "We've been standing here for ten minutes." Her words were slurred and angry, and she waved her empty glass in his face. "Do you know how dehydrated a person can get in that amount of time?"

"Think Karen Carpenter," the blonde threw at him.

"Oh, sweetie." The dark-haired one looked at her. "Do you remember when I did that PR thing for her? Do you remember what that was, darling?"

"Her funeral," the other said matter-of-factly.

"God, what a depressing time that was." She hung her head low. "We lost a bloody fortune on those gorgeous little thimble things with her ashes in them. I don't know why people wouldn't buy them."

"It worked for Mount St. Helens," the blonde added crassly.

"Exactly! Only there was a whole lot more ash there. By the time we got her here, there was barely enough to bother with. Anyway, cheers, sweetie!" The heavier one lifted her glass and then remembered it was empty.

"Would you like me to fill that for you, madam?" The waiter lifted the bottle up, ready to pour some into their glasses.

"Moiselle," the blonde chastised him. "Made-*moiselle!*"

"Just give us the bottle and leave." The heavier one grabbed the bottle and poured some for herself and then her friend. The waiter, not knowing what else to do, left in search of another bottle to carry around.

I was about to turn and leave as well when the woman turned and looked at me.

"You look a bit dry there yourself. Here." She thrust the bottle into my hand. "Oh, look!" The blonde turned towards the food table. "Are those Japanese finger foods?"

The two women stumbled off toward the buffet tables, and I took the opportunity to head in the opposite direction toward the blessed absence of humanity. It probably wouldn't do my stomach much good to drink without filling it first, but I couldn't see it necessarily hurting, either.

It turned out the yard was a bit larger than I had first thought. All I wanted to do was find the farthest corner and sit down, but the closer I got to the side of the house the more surprised I was to see that the yard was opening up again. Far away from everyone else's sight was a kind of side yard with a few tables and chairs, regular lawn furniture, really. I doubt it was meant to be used for the party, but it certainly looked inviting enough to me.

I fell lazily into a lounger, kicked my feet up and took a long swig from the bottle. This was heaven!

"Get that out of your mouth!" a voice rang out. "You're not old enough to be drinking!"

The entire contents sprayed simultaneously out through my mouth and nose. I was going to kick the living shit out of whoever just scared me like that! The burning in my nose was almost worse than what I'd felt in my groin before it had gone numb in the car.

Somebody laughed and handed me a couple of napkins. By God, they weren't going to be laughing when I got a hold of the son of a...

As quickly as my still-convulsing body would let me, I stood up and turned around to face the object of my aggressions.

"I'm sorry." I felt a hand dab at my face with a fresh napkin. "That really wasn't very nice of me, but I couldn't resist."

I finally managed to see through the deep hue my body had turned and get a clear view of the face before me. Incredible! It was as if I was looking at myself in a mirror, only a little older and a whole lot better-looking.

He was in his early twenties, and had light blond hair, clear blue eyes and picture-perfect Don Johnson *Miami Vice*-style hair. I'd tried for years to get *my* hair to do anything—anything at all—but I had too many cowlicks.

We were about the same height, but he had a physique that was a bit more appealing to the eyes than my own.

I completely forgot for the moment what he had just done to me but still hated him.

He extended his hand and, instead of punching him, my own met his. I *wanted* to punch him. I *tried* to get my hand to punch him, but my body betrayed me! Despite how hot under the collar I was feeling, I felt the warmth of his skin against mine, and I think I actually blushed. It had to be the alcohol.

"My name's Jordan." He introduced himself, and I still wanted to hurt him, now more than ever. What kind of name was that, anyway? Playboys were named Jordan, the kind who acted as though they invented sex and then tried like hell to spread it around. He was the epitome of why I couldn't get a date. How could I compete with a name and look like that? "What's yours?"

"I'm Marie and Donald's son," I told him, defeated and still dribbling champagne from my mouth and nostrils.

"Is that what you want me to call you?" He looked a bit puzzled. "Do you have a really difficult foreign name or something? I'm fluent in four languages, so I'm sure I could give it a try pronouncing it."

"No." God, he made me sick! Four languages? I'll bet I had him beat. I knew English, British, Australian, Profane, and I could probably get by if I had to in the realm of Love. That made five! He wasn't such hot shit after all. "It's just that nobody can seem to remember my name. So far, I've been called Adam, Alex, Axel, Amos, Abner and Butch. If, however, you can ignore everybody else's interpretations, it's really just Andy."

That sounded so plain. Jordan was the kind of name some girl took home to meet her billionaire parents and to get memberships for at exclusive health clubs and dining clubs. Andy was the kind of name parents hired to entertain their children when the television wasn't on.

"That's an easy name to remember."

He said it so simply and honestly that I almost believed him. Then again, why shouldn't I believe him? Of course it was an easy name to remember! It didn't need a masters degree, though I'm sure he had one of those, too.

"In fact, there's a number of famous people with that name."

"Really?" I heard myself ask him, and then realized I might have actually sounded sincere. Where was my uncanny sense of sarcasm? Why was my mouth boycotting any effort I made to tell him to go dance naked in a pit of fiery hot coals and burn? "How would you know?"

There went another brilliant effort on my part.

"Get real!" Jordan playfully hit me in the arm, and I wished for a chainsaw and a copy of the movie *Scarface*. "This is California, home of *Hollywood*." He raised his hands to the sky to accent the word. "Actually, I was thinking of someone more involved with music than acting or the movies." He moved around to a chair next to the lounger I had been lying on and sat down. "Andy Taylor. He's the—"

"Ex-guitar player from Duran Duran." I finished the sentence for him and sat back down on the lounger. My God, he actually knew who Andy

Taylor was!

"Who had songs on three soundtracks and then also released two solo albums..." Jordan stopped and looked at me, probably to see if I could fill in any of the blanks. So, this was a test.

"The soundtracks being *American Anthem*, *Miami Vice 2* and *Tequila Sunrise* and then the solo albums *Thunder* and *Dangerous*." I wasn't stupid, however, and he was missing something.

"*Dangerous* being a bunch of cover songs...."

"And only available on Japanese import. Of course, you *are* neglecting his involvement with Power Station." I returned a playful punch to his arm, and Jordan nodded his head as if I'd added the one thing he wasn't going to handfeed me. I actually felt pleased about it, though I couldn't figure out why. Maybe I had just been looking for an excuse to wrinkle his clothes and make him a little less perfect than he was.

"Wow! I thought I was the only person in the world who knew who he was and listened to his music."

"Are you kidding?" Jordan sighed and looked down at the ground. I looked, too, but didn't see anything out of the ordinary. There was just grass, and not the kind anyone smoked. Just green grass...

I looked harder. It didn't smell of any chemicals or anything people have sprayed on their lawn. No, it was just grass. What the hell was he looking at?

Jordan didn't move for another minute, and I wondered if he had just simply run out his batteries or something. Finally, he raised his head and looked me straight in the eye.

"So, are you family?"

"Aren't we all?" I laughed. I mean, why else would we be here? Why else would I have been here? In some cases, duty, but not mine. Duty was why I stayed, not why I originally came. Well, duty and the fact I didn't have a ride back to the airport or an earlier plane ticket back home. Only family could put each other through so much in so little time.

"It'd be great if we all were." He gave me a sly look. "But I don't think that's the way it is, at least, not here."

"Okay." What more could I say than that? In one respect, I could see if my great-aunt and -uncle wanted to celebrate their fiftieth wedding anniversary with family only. After all, it was a very special occasion and landmark in their lives. On the other hand, I could also understand them wanting to share it with their closest friends, too. It didn't really matter so long as they were having a good time and celebrating it the way they wanted.

"Well, I guess they have to have friends, too."

Maybe Jordan was just trying to feel me out, to see if I had a snobby attitude about others being here. He could be a neighbor's son who was invited and been given dirty looks all night because he wasn't a blood relative. It seemed stupid to me he would think I would hold it against him just because he wasn't a cousin or someone like that. Considering how I felt about my relatives lately, I was likely to be warmer and *more* considerate to him than any of them.

"I'm family anyway."

"Cool!" Jordan winked and looked me over from

head to toe. The only thing I could come up with was that he was trying to place which side of the family I belonged to, but since I looked more like my father than my mother, I doubted he'd figure it out anytime soon.

His reaction struck me as a little odd, even rude and a bit invasive, but then, maybe that was the way people were out here. Being so close to Hollywood, one's appearance was everything, and it was probably scrutinized by bums on the street as well as friends and relatives. Jordan was most likely just doing what he naturally always did.

"So, how long have you been out?"

"Since a couple of hours ago." The way he phrased his question struck me a little odd as well. Again, it must just be a California thing. If he could look me over and not be the least bit uncomfortable while doing it, then he probably felt unhindered in speaking to me in fluent Californease. As far as I was concerned, that was a positive thing; and to show that I was willing to embrace his culture, I looked him over from head to toe, too.

"That recent?" Jordan seemed both genuinely surprised and pleased at the same time. How queer.

"Well, traveling these days doesn't take nearly as long as it used to. I think we made it here in four hours. Tack on a few hours to get luggage and then drive here...I'd say I've been out seven hours now."

"What?" He appeared confused. I thought I'd kept my response simple enough, but maybe I'd said too much. Dad used to say that I loved talking just to hear myself talk. I hoped that wasn't what I was doing now because the last thing I wanted to do was lose him in the conversation, especially since he and I were relating to each other so wonderfully. "No," he continued, "I meant how long have you been *out*?"

Well, *that* cleared things up...

"Since..." I didn't quite know what he meant, now, and I hated to give the wrong answer. "I left Detroit, like I just told you. I'm not quite sure what you're asking."

Something caught my attention, coming from behind me. It was like I felt the presence of someone else watching me, only it wasn't quite as mystical an experience as what might have been felt in, say, *Star Wars*. I can only describe it as suddenly picking up on changes in the surrounding air density, a kind of radar thing.

I turned around and saw two people I recognized as my homosexual cousins standing there. They peered at me. One of them seemed as though he was getting ready to speak, but before he could, I turned back around and faced Jordan. I hoped it didn't look too rude—just as long as they got the idea I was already conversing with someone and didn't care to be interrupted.

A few seconds passed, and I turned back around. They were gone.

"Whew!" That was a close call.

"What's the matter?" Jordan asked playfully. It was unnerving how charming he could be even saying the simplest things. I'll bet he had other guys quaking in their shoes when he was angry and made women weep when he cried. He would, of course, be the kind of guy who wasn't afraid to wear his emotions on his sleeve, especially when there were women around. They ate that crap up, and his tears would probably only add to their desire to have him and hold him, soothe him, maybe, and definitely have sex with him. Most guys I knew only cried so they could use the salt from the tears on someone's open wound. They could be sadistic that way.

"They're..."

I don't know why, but I just didn't want to say the word in front of Jordan. It seemed a personal thing to discuss, and that topic had never really come up with any of my friends in general conversation, so I wasn't comfortable with it. The only time the word got used was when people called me that in high school, or when women figured it was the reason I didn't want to have sex. I knew how it sounded being spoken to me, and I just didn't want to make it sound that way now. Just because I didn't agree with the lifestyle didn't mean I couldn't be tactful.

"*You* know..." My discomfort was obvious, but he appeared as though he expected me to finish my statement anyway. "Okay, they're..." I spoke slowly, hoping he would catch on. "...the festive sort, lively and happy."

Nothing. He was playing stupid. He had to be!

"Uh...joyous."

"You mean gay?" he asked matter-of-factly, and I winced. The word rolled off his tongue so easily I wondered if he had been one of those people who tormented others about their sexuality and called them that name. At least he hadn't called *me* that.

Then, too, with real gay people around, it should be obvious I wasn't one of them, so why would he?

"Well, yeah, gay is as good a word as any other, I guess—that whole gay/happy thing." I think I was blushing again.

He was still looking at me in that same playful way when I began to notice for the first time just how smooth his face was and how completely un-blemished and perfect his features were. Jordan didn't have a protruding or underdeveloped chin, an oversized or undersized nose or uneven eyes. It was as if his parents had their ideal child formatted or put together on a birthing computer and he was what it delivered as the end result.

I used to wonder what it would be like to be someone—well, someone like him. I wondered how it would feel to be so damn perfect-looking and be able to catch a glimpse of myself in the mirror in the morning and not frown. All those curiosities went away one day when I realized I should stop thinking about them because I would never know. That would never be me, not without plastic surgery.

"I mean, it doesn't bother me like it does a lot of other people."

"What other people?" Jordan looked around us. "This is California."

"Maybe some people are a bit more liberal in this state." I chuckled dryly. "But not my relatives—at least, not the ones I've talked to." The champagne was looking very inviting again. I took a long drink from the bottle. "I think it's in the language." I took another drink and then looked him right in the eye. "The word *gay* should be replaced with *happy* or something with a less negative connotative meaning attached to it. How can anyone say anything bad about someone being happy?" I felt I had a very valid point, and I'd certainly rather be asked if I was happy than gay.

I took yet another drink, and then figured I should stop, especially since the champagne was making me warm all over again. The stuff went through me quicker than any other alcohol I'd ever had.

"It's just that, words like *homosexual*—who wants to be one of those? If someone wants a little diversity, call them a person who's happy, because everybody else in life is pretty damn miserable. But, call them a homosexual? It's in the name, see?" I shook my head. "It really doesn't matter, anyway. I'm no more a homosexual than you are."

"Actually..." Jordan eyed the near-empty bottle and then me again. "I *am* a homosexual."

He must have seen the confused expression come over my face because he suddenly felt the need to clarify.

"I'm gay—'happy.'"

"No." I laughed nervously. "You're not."

He was playing a joke on me. He had to be. You could never take people like him seriously.

"Yes, I am," Jordan insisted.

"No, you're *not*," I informed him.

"Why not?"

"You can't be!" It was really just that simple.

"Why?"

"Because." Why was he making this so difficult? Why didn't he just admit that he was pulling my leg? Enough was enough.

"Because why?" Jordan looked at me with a sincerity that made me suddenly realize he might be telling the truth.

My first feeling was devastation, but I didn't explore it very much and found it far more comfortable to revert back to denial. Such disturbing and severe emotions didn't need attention until it was absolutely necessary.

"Why?" I searched my mind for an answer to his question. Did I really have one? "Because...you know who Andy Taylor is." Other words and reasons escaped my mind. "Um...because you don't look like one." He didn't, either. He wasn't in his thirties or forties or ugly as sin and didn't have a mustache or any tattoos that I could see. He was just like me, only better-looking.

"Oh, please." Jordan rolled his eyes. "Don't tell me you're one of those people holding on to the stereotypes that all gay men are in their thirties and forties, are butt-ugly, have mustaches and tattoos, are you?"

"Of course not." Now *I* rolled *my* eyes. "I mean, what kind of person do you think I am, anyway?" I turned, snorted then looked back at him. "I'm a writer," I explained. "As a breed, we hate cliches and stereotypes. You just seem normal, that's all."

I never would have guessed or suspected it about him. Why did he have to tell me he was gay? I mean, why ruin such a perfect conversation with talk like that? Maybe he was just trying to be interesting. If so, he didn't need to be. I was perfectly captivated with him the way he was.

"You look...normal." I spoke the word again.

"What's normal?" Jordan had obviously had this conversation with others before because he knew exactly what to say to stump me at every turn.

"I've never been asked that before." I thought about what to say to him. I felt like I owed him an answer, mostly because it seemed like something he needed to hear. Or was that me who needed to hear it? If so, then why? "I guess normal is a stereotype in itself. If you were a stereotypical gay, then you would look and act a very certain way that would define you as a 'normal' gay. If you were a yuppie, you would look and act in another very specific way. While there's going to be some differences from person to person, there will always be similarities. Now that I think about it, maybe it's the similarities that define the norm."

I was confusing *myself*. There really didn't seem to be a solid definition of normal that I had a grasp of. God, did anybody? I wondered how well Jordan knew himself. It was time to find out.

"Let me put this a different way. How do you know you're gay?" I asked him, straightforward and matter-of-factly.

"How do you know you're straight?" he retorted in the same manner.

"Well..." *Well, shit! That backfired.* I had absolutely no idea what made me think I was straight. Could that be his point? And why was he smiling at me?

If I could tell him how I knew I was straight, I would be answering my own question to him. If I could "just know," then it would follow that he could, too, unless he was lying.

"Let me put it another way."

I wasn't going to let him know I was wrestling with the answer. The last thing I wanted to reveal was that he might actually have me on this whole issue so far. I hated it when the beautiful people got the upper hand with me.

"When did you first fantasize you were gay?"

"Fantasize?" Jordan gazed at me.

"Realize. I said realize." I hoped my face didn't give away that I just realized I really had said "fantasize."

"Right."

Okay, so he wasn't buying it. I tried.

"When did *you* first realize you were straight?"

"What?" Prick! Would he quit doing that?

I supposed my answer should have been along the lines of knowing it when I first lay with a woman and had sex with her, but that hadn't exactly happened yet. He didn't need to know that, though. The last time I'd been with anybody— actually, the *only* times I'd been with anybody— had been my guy friends back home a long time ago. Jordan didn't need to know *that*, either, since I didn't think it would help my case much.

"I feel like I'm having a conversation with myself here." That wasn't too far from the truth.

"Maybe that's a good thing." He spoke softly, and looked at me with knowing eyes. Exactly what it was they knew was beyond me, but something was going through that mind of his I wasn't privy to. It was just a little unnerving.

"Maybe you've needed to have this conversation with yourself for a long time. I know a lot of people who have."

Jordan suddenly tried to sound reassuring.

"What?" I hoped that response wasn't about to become habitual, since it was the second time I'd spoken it. What, exactly, was going on here? Jordan knew what conversations people had to have? What in the hell did he mean by that? For that matter, what good was it doing asking *myself* what he meant? "What do you mean by that?" Well, it was a start. "Not that I'm gay, I hope, 'cause I'm not. I like women."

It wasn't exactly a lie. I did like women. I just hadn't found the one I wanted to engage in nocturnal mating rituals with.

"Do you?" He spoke the words evenly and without giving away whatever it was he was thinking. It was hardly fair.

"Very much so." I needed to convince him of this. My situation of never having been with a woman sexually might open up doors of conversation and thought I wasn't ready to defend myself in. I didn't have any real experiences to draw from, but I certainly had a number of other people's. "I'm into the whole...trapeze bar-from-the-ceiling thing."

It was the only thing I could think of. All the things my roommate Todd used to tell me about, and I couldn't remember a single one of them.

"I've hosted a number of orgies. I like women. I love that..." I knew I would blush if I said the word. "...area between their legs, especially when they shave it." Finally, I'd said something I remembered from Todd. "Sometimes, I have a couple of them every night."

"Wow!" Jordan paused and seemed to consider what I'd said. "I'm impressed."

It was difficult to tell if he was being sincere or not. I don't know why, but I had the distinct impression he wasn't exactly believing everything I told him. Was it the way I was saying it, or was it what I was saying?

"I hope you get tested."

"Tested?"

What the hell kind of shit was this? Is that what gay guys did? Test each other during sex? What did two guys do in bed that required testing, anyway? Did they have scorecards and markers next to the bed and rate every performance?

"You mean have them grade me?"

He couldn't seriously expect me to believe that straight couples did the same thing. Oh, Christ, what if they did? Had some part of me always known I would be graded? Maybe the real pros didn't need grading, but I was hardly a pro. I didn't even think I rated as an amateur.

"Give me a break! I go to school. Those are all the tests I can handle."

"No." Jordan chuckled. "I mean testing as in for sexually transmitted diseases. Since you're with so many women, I assume you want to remain safe."

"Oh, that. Well, yeah!" Maybe I did have some hang-ups I needed to get rid of. Maybe I needed to take another health class while I was at it, too, and catch up on everything I didn't seem to know.

Just exactly how did one get tested to know if they were safe or not? I'd never had to worry about it, so I never really paid much attention. Ignorance wasn't an excuse. I suppose if it fell off, I'd know I had a problem.

I really needed that health class.

"Yeah, I'm into that whole testing thing. In fact, I get tested at least once a week for DV."

"DV?" he asked. "Are you nervous? Don't you mean VD?"

"Veterinarial disease...whatever." Why would he think I was nervous? I didn't think I was nervous so where did he get off thinking it? Damn it! I wasn't nervous! I just didn't have any clue what I was talking about, that's all.

Well, okay, maybe I was a little bit on edge. It wasn't every day I had a one-on-one talk with a homosexual, and an attractive one at that. I didn't know they came that way. At least now it made a little more sense why he was looking me over earlier.

Actually, no, it didn't. With the exception of the one girl in high school, I hadn't been able to get a girl to give me a *first* look, much less a second one; and I refused to believe that men were the only ones who found me attractive. What if they were, though? That could be a bad thing because I didn't think I was gay...

No, I knew I wasn't gay. I couldn't be.

"Look, that's not important here." I looked him straight in the eye. "What I'm not trying to tell you is that I'm gay." That didn't sound right. "No, what I'm trying to tell you is that I'm not gay—that's what I'm trying to tell you."

"I never said you were." Jordan eyed me in what appeared to be mock sympathy. Again, I had the feeling he thought he knew something I didn't.

"And I like women," I repeated.

"I never said you didn't." He laughed.

"And trapeze bars." He shouldn't forget that.

"That's a little strange, even for me." He gave me another playful nudge on the arm, as if to say that things were understood and accepted between us. "Mostly *I* like to cuddle, hold hands, listen to music, share a gourmet dinner on the beach and watch the sunset with a bottle of fine wine..."

His voice trailed off, and I found myself actually enjoying the mood he was setting. There was nothing unusual about it at all. They were all the things I had always wanted with a partner, only never had. Most of the guys I knew would never admit to wanting to share those things with their girlfriends, so I found it ironic that I would be hearing it now from someone who was gay. With the guys from school, it was just sex, sex, sex. But here...

"...and," Jordan continued, and I listened intently, hanging on his next few words and the place they would take me, "when the time is right, make hot, passionate love."

Nope, I definitely wasn't going to that place.

"I've never been able to get into this whole carefree sex thing, like trapeze bars and orgies. It's too seventies for a guy like me."

"Well." I tried to sound like a typical male who was admitting something he shouldn't. "Let me tell you—sex is kinda overrated. All that strange stuff is fine and all, but it's not exactly what I would call fulfilling."

I wondered if typical men ever even used the word *fulfilling*, but Jordan nodded as if he understood what I was saying. Well, he would. I had absolutely no idea if sex was overrated or not, but I really did identify with all the things he said he wanted to share with a partner.

"Sometimes, I find myself just wanting to spend time with someone and talk about what's going on in life, about what's going on in their life and my own. I want to share my ideas about what I'm writing, what I want to write, maybe read a poem and have them give me some feedback. I want to hear about their day and, if it was good, share the happiness and, if it was bad, help cheer them up or share in their sorrow." I looked up at him. "You know?"

"I know."

"I don't ever want to limit myself or settle."

There wasn't much space between the two of us, and I was suddenly grateful for that. What I was saying was personal, and I felt as if he was the one person who could understand me right now. Maybe it was because he didn't mind me talking or because he actually seemed interested in what I had to say, but I felt I could identify with him, and I didn't pretend to understand why. It was just a good feeling and I went with my instincts.

"Unfortunately, I sometimes set my standards so high that no one can ever live up to them, but I still won't settle."

"I don't ever want to settle, either," he said in soft agreement.

"Then, too, maybe it's more than that for me. Sometimes, I feel like I'm one of those idiots who's so busy trying to conquer the world, but who creates so many other problems in the process that I end up losing myself in the struggle to keep myself out of trouble."

The grass suddenly seemed very appealing to look at, and I lowered my head to stare at it.

"Then, sometimes, I think the reason I do that is so I can lose myself. I've never really thought much of myself, and with the exception of my parents, no one else ever has, either. It's just something I've learned to live with instead of constantly feeling sorry for myself. I could end up a very lonely and bitter old man one day." I looked back up and stared into his eyes. "Only that's not what I want.

"The more I try to lose myself, though, the faster I find myself running from everything and everyone. I don't want to miss out on friendships and romance with the right people, but I don't know how to slow down long enough to take a look around me."

"Maybe someone should slow you down." Jordan leaned forward and kissed me. It was only a light brushing of the lips, but it was enough to substantiate its being called a kiss. *Why did he do that?*

"Why did you do that?"

Everything felt suddenly still, as if nothing else existed around us. I wondered if this moment was somehow being frozen in time, but to what end? Jordan, this man I just met and had opened up to, had kissed me. I had never romantically kissed a man in my life, even when I was experimenting with my friends so many years ago. Actually, I still hadn't kissed a man romantically. *He* kissed *me*, not vice-versa!

I didn't know how I felt about this, mostly because I think the spirits had gotten to me. The champagne was really making me sweat, and my entire body felt like it was on fire. Hell, my lips were tingling. This was some expensive stuff!

"Because I wanted to and you wanted me to."

"No, I didn't." I backed away a little bit in case he thought about doing it again. No more alcohol for me! My body felt like it was melting right into the lounger, and my mind seemed to be reaching for some euphoric state I dared not escape to yet. "Why would you get the idea I wanted you to kiss me? I just got done telling you I liked women. So, why did you do it?"

"I told you, you wanted me to."

"I did not! I never said 'Jordan, kiss me.'"

"Now you're just saying it verbally." He moved towards me again, and I moved farther away.

"Don't do it again!" I fell backwards off the lounger. "Shit!" I quickly stood back up, however unsteadily. "It's bad enough you did it the first time."

He seemed to be enjoying the entire scenario.

"What? You think I *enjoyed* it?"

"Well..." He motioned with his head and eyes at my waist. "...you tell me."

"Huh?" I looked down and saw the problem. I'd been so preoccupied with the current events that I hadn't realized just how claustrophobic my pants had grown. "It's the champagne."

I just wanted to get away, mostly to cover up the fact I had an erection. Whatever was going on and whatever reactions I was having to the situation simply didn't feel right. I couldn't identify specifically what they were, but they made me very uncomfortable.

Why was he doing this to me?

"Look, uh, it's been nice talking to you, but I know there's a relative of mine here..." I started walking backwards. "...who I thought was dead but isn't." I put my hand in my pocket to try and correct a rather protruding problem. "And I have to talk to her before she does die and before I leave in sex days...*six* days."

Jordan looked after me, still amused.

"It's really a nasty thing, too, because she's extremely old and..." I backed up farther. "...her flesh is practically falling off her bones. Pretty soon, nobody'll be able to understand what she's talking about because her mouth will be hanging right where her breasts used to be."

5

The rest of the party was a total disaster. The first thing I did after leaving Jordan and the side yard was to adjust myself and head over to where the food was and fix a plate. It was of paramount importance to me that I counteract the effects of the champagne, especially since I still wasn't thinking very clearly.

There was still a bit of a line at the buffet table, but I finally managed to start picking up some little delicacies. Best of all, no one thought to talk to me, and that precluded any stress of having to make pleasant and banal conversation back. I was too stressed out anyway. Thinking about the kiss—and the fact I'd had an erection—wasn't the tough part. Thinking about not thinking about the kiss and erection was the trick. That was what made things so stressful.

All the times in my life when I pulled a boner, and here I actually had one.

The more I thought about it, though, the more it stayed. If I tried not to think about it, I ended up thinking about it anyway, mostly because I was hoping to God no one saw it. I had to think about something else, something that was unrelated to anything currently going on.

"Oh, wow!" The woman next to me exclaimed and tapped on my shoulder. "What are those little things there on your plate?"

"Uh..." I turned to face her and almost jumped out of my skin! As much as I was trying not to think about sex, there in front of me was a blonde in her thirties scantily clad in one of the tightest, most revealing excuses for a dress I'd ever seen. To make matters worse, she was incredibly well-endowed. "They're rib tits..." I couldn't help but look at them, but I quickly realized my faux pas. "Tips! Sorry, rib tips." I tried to laugh it off.

"Where did you get them?" she asked, politely pretending to ignore my little slip. After all, anyone wearing a dress like that had to know they were going to draw attention to themselves. "I think they ran out of cheese sticks, and those look like the next best thing."

"Um, well, you must have missed them. They were back with the breast of the meat." I shook my head. God, I was looking like an ass! "Rest...of the meat. Long night." I hoped she didn't come with a boyfriend or husband who would twist my little girly man self up into a pretzel after talking to her that way. Why did she have to talk to me in the first place? Didn't she know? Couldn't she see how red and nervous I was?

I attempted some sort of explanation. "I–I apologize. I just don't get out very often, and my social graces are a bit busty...lusty...*rusty*! Look..." I pointed somewhere behind her. "...there's Rusty."

94

She turned to look, too. "Oh, damn, he disappeared into the house." My recovery sucked! "I better go look for him."

"Have you been drinking?" She caught my shoulder with her hand.

"Yeah, it, uh...it shows, doesn't it? I'm a little titsy...tipsy." I put my hand up so she wouldn't say another word. We were both aware I was making a royal asshole out of myself, but I didn't want her to publicly acknowledge it because I had no intentions of being around anybody else the rest of the night.

At that moment, Jordan and my two homosexual cousins walked up and stood in line. That didn't bother me, but Jordan looked at me and winked. I had to get out of there!

"I'm just going to go inside and see if I can scare up a waiter to bring you out some more of those cheese dicks...sticks."

This night sucked!

❈ ❈ ❈

I spent the rest of the evening either out on the front porch or inside the house in one of the guest rooms watching *The Golden Girls* on TV. Maybe I was feeling a bit sorry for myself, because I didn't feel I could rejoin the party and have a good time. How in the hell did my vacation suddenly become so complicated?

I only had one issue getting on that plane and that was my virginity. I wanted to lose it! However, losing it to a guy was not foremost on my wish list.

I really didn't want to deal with that right now.

I would poke my head out every once in a while and find Grandma, make sure she was okay and try and determine what time we were leaving so I would know when to come out. Finally, about midnight, the four of us crammed back into Uncle Chester's economy car and headed back to their place. This time, however, *I* arranged the suitcase on my lap.

"That was an absolutely gorgeous party!" Grandma remarked once we were back on the freeway. I think we all would have enjoyed silence, but she was probably worried Uncle Chester would fall asleep at the wheel. "Leon and Carma looked so happy. Actually, everybody looked happy."

"That's because they were all drinking to forget their troubles and had amnesia by the end of the night," I commented, overtired and ornery.

"Don't you dare get insolent!" Grandma snapped. "You don't know what you're talking about!" It was easier to dismiss me this way than admit some people actually had problems. "Those people are adults and have taken care of themselves for years. A little drink at a party isn't going to hurt anyone."

"A little drink?" Who was she kidding? Probably herself, because she was toasted. "Grandma, the shortest distance those people were traveling from any given place was two pints. As far as taking care of themselves, if it wasn't for the slivers of fruit, cherries and olives, some of them would have starved to death."

"You know, Anson..." Uncle Chester sternly looked over at me. "...you're the reason why adults in this country used to hold the rule that 'children should be seen and not heard' so dearly."

How did his wife ever put up with him? She didn't drink. In fact, I think Aunt Virginia and I were the two people at the party who were sober. I only had soft drinks after the incident with Jordan.

Well, I had no intention of fighting with him, even though I had a comeback and the urge to make it verbal. He and Aunt Virginia were putting us up at their place for the night. At least, I think it was only for the night. To be honest, I hadn't thought that far ahead. We were going to be in California for six days, and I had no idea what the arrangements were.

This wasn't good.

Sometime later—I don't know how long it had been because I'd dozed off—we entered Sun City and pulled into the driveway of what looked to be one of the newer houses in the subdivision, which itself looked new. From what I could see by the streetlights, none of the houses looked the same, but all were extremely impressive in their architecture. They weren't mansions, by any means, but they were unique for what I guessed to be a retirement community.

I wondered what Uncle Chester had done for a job during his working years to be able to afford a place like this. It had the potential to really be something grand, and I say *potential* because the area was still new. Lawns and landscaping had yet to be finished, and there was still quite a few dirt piles to be taken care of, especially in Uncle Chester's front yard.

"You behave yourself around your grandmother tonight," He ordered after taking me aside while Grandma followed Aunt Virginia up the sidewalk to the front door. "There's no reason you need to be acting like a scallop."

"Scamp." I was too tired to put up with this. "The

word is *scamp*."

"Keep it up, Arnold."

I followed him into the house. He promised to show Grandma and me around the place the next day, since she wanted to get to bed before her face fell off. That was kind of a twist on something I heard she always said in the morning.

Whenever she first got up, Grandma complained she had to go put her face on so she looks presentable. Uncle Chester must have noticed that the excitement of the party and exposure to the California environment were causing her makeup to come unglued. I wondered what she looked like without makeup. Did she have natural beauty, or was it the lack of it that made her "put on a face" each and every day?

The inside of the house was spacious and open, but there weren't as many rooms as I would have expected. There was a large living room upon entering, with a dining area and kitchen off to the left. No walls separated the areas, which I guessed made things convenient for parties and other social functions. In some ways, I guess it was simplicity and utility all in one.

The master bedroom was off the kitchen, and the guestroom was off the living room with a guest bathroom between them. Each bedroom had a bathroom with a bathtub, too, which was a nice addition to the room. It reminded me of a hotel, for some reason, except that the lamps and pictures weren't nailed down.

"Wow!" I commented on seeing the king-sized bed in the guestroom as I set my suitcase down.

"Why are you putting that in here?" Grandma

asked me, uncertainty written all over her face, or what was left of it.

"What do you mean?" Why wouldn't I bring my suitcase in the room with us? There was plenty of room for all three of them.

"Leave it out in the living room where you're sleeping." She actually looked annoyed now. Worse yet, I had the feeling she really believed I was going to be sleeping out there.

"I'm not sleeping out there." I looked out into the living room. The only thing besides a couple of chairs that didn't recline was a couch that seated two at the most. "This is a king-sized bed...a *king-sized*," I emphasized, "and that couch out there wouldn't sleep a court jester comfortably. Now, you can put up an electric fence down the middle of the bed that delivers a fatal shock upon an attempted transgression, but we're going to have to share."

I really wasn't in the mood to argue about this. I didn't care if she thought it was weird or sick that a grandmother and her grandson share a king-sized bed or not. I was tired, and all I wanted to do was sleep. We could argue about it in the morning.

"All right."

I couldn't believe it. This was a first. Maybe she was too tired to put up much of a fight, but she had actually given in. I mean, this was progress!

"Would you please at least take your suitcase in the other room so we can walk in here without it being too cramped?"

"Absolutely." I was only too eager to perform this minor concession, even though I didn't think we would be that cramped. Still, I was getting something I wanted, so I didn't mind doing

99

something she wanted.

This was how things were supposed to work. There was no law or rule saying that two people couldn't logically figure something out that benefited both. Both of us needed a good night's sleep, and I would get that. What would she be getting out of this, though? Nothing.

I picked the suitcase up and carried it into the living room. This wasn't like her, not at all. It seemed a bit odd to me that she would give in so easily when it didn't benefit her in any way.

Ker-chunk. Click.

"Grandma?" There was no reply. I turned around and saw that the door was closed. In fact, I think she'd locked it, too. If she was going to get changed, why didn't she just use the bathroom?

Maybe because she had no intention of sharing the room with me in the first place.

"Grandma?" I knocked twice on the door. Again, no reply. Maybe that was because she had no intention of replying just as she had no intention of letting me sleep in the king-sized bed. Bitch locked me out!

I raised both fists in utter frustration and mocked pounding on the door. A small noise distracted me, and I turned around to find Aunt Virginia staring at me, standing there with both of my fists still raised in a rather unusual display of the brutality I was feeling. Her eyes grew wider than I think I've ever seen on a human being before, and she dropped a pillow and some sheets on the floor as she turned and hightailed it back to her bedroom.

"Well, shit," I mumbled and went over to pick up

what she had dropped. I barely had a chance to speak to the woman all night, and then she catches me in the middle of a quiet temper tantrum. This was once again not how I had envisioned things happening on my vacation.

The couch wasn't exactly what I had envisioned, either. To someone who stood six feet tall, their couch seemed more like a loveseat than something to be used to sleep on. I checked to see if it folded out into a bed. It didn't. Swell.

I shook my head, got changed in the bathroom, brushed my teeth and lay down. The most I could do was either lie with my feet hanging off the end or curl up in a fetal position. To make matters worse, the cushions on the back of the couch were so puffy it made turning over without falling off the damn thing nearly impossible.

"Oh, well." I closed my eyes and prayed for sleep to take me quickly.

Tick-tock, tick-tock, tick-tock, tick-tock...

"Nooo..." One eye opened and scanned the room for that obnoxious noise. I finally saw the enemy, and it was closer than I had initially imagined. At the far end of the couch, near my feet and against the wall, was a fully functional grandfather clock. Now, I'd seen grandfather clocks that were quiet and inconspicuous, but of course, my aunt and uncle would have to choose the one most likely to sound like a Charles Bronson movie in progress. If I dreamt about a time bomb going off and woke up screaming in the middle of the night, at least I would know why.

Why not just open the thing up and stop it? It should be a simple enough procedure. But then I'd have to explain my actions in the morning, and I didn't even want to think about what Uncle Chester would say to me then.

What's the matter? Little girly ears can't take a little clock? I suppose you're one of those kids who can't take the Snap! Crackle! Pop! of Rice Krispies in the morning, either. Wanna wear some earplugs at breakfast in case the toaster is too loud?

"Ohhhh..." I moaned at the thought. The annoyance of the clock could never compare to the annoyance of that man berating me and treating me like he did. Was he that way with everybody my age? My cousins were older than I was, but I wondered if he treated them the same way, especially because they were gay. How would he treat Jordan? Hell, I wondered how he would treat me if he thought I was gay.

Now there was an entertaining thought. Tomorrow morning I could always just announce at the breakfast table that I'd had my first kiss last night at the party and decided I couldn't lie to myself anymore, or anybody else, for that matter. That would certainly get me on a plane for home a whole lot sooner than I'd expected.

I shuddered as a mental picture of Jordan leaning forward to kiss me flashed through my mind. Why had he done that? Who else had he done that with this evening? My cousins? Some part of me wondered who he was in bed with tonight. Again, one of my cousins? What the hell did people like them do in bed, anyway?

It wasn't any of my business. What really made me sick was that, even though he was gay, he was probably having more sex than I ever would. It seemed everybody was. I really needed to get to sleep before I started feeling sorry for myself again.

Ding-ding-ding-ding, ding-ding-ding-ding!

"You have got to be fucking kidding?" I hissed. What the hell time was it, anyway? Since it was obvious I wasn't going to get much sleep, I sat up and turned on a light. It was two-thirty in the morning. Great, it was set to go off on the half-hour as well as the hour. I could hardly wait to hear what that sounded like. Well, I'd find out in thirty minutes.

I turned the light off, put the pillow over my head and tried desperately to go to sleep without committing a homicide or act of vandalism to my aunt and uncle's property.

※ ※ ※

The bright California sun beat unmercifully down upon my bronzed skin, but it didn't burn me. It couldn't even touch me through the suntan lotion five young blond women in string bikinis were gently massaging into my legs, arms, back and neck. Their own skin was tanned to the peak of perfection, which only matched the beauty of their faces and figures. They were perfect, the most perfect women I'd ever laid eyes on.

All five women giggled in some shared moment of happiness at being with and pleasing me. I knew what they were hoping for, and I knew they didn't think they would all get it, but they would. I would let each and every one of them have a piece of me right there on the beach with the sound of the ocean crashing upon the shore as our music and our moans the lyrics of our passion.

These were California women, the liveliest,

prettiest and horniest of all women in the world...except French women, but they didn't shave under their arms, so they didn't count.

One of them rolled me over on my beach towel and started rubbing lotion into my chest, which was miraculously far more muscular than I had ever seen it before. This was a me I could get used to. I was now a hardbody!

Well, that was the term I'd heard used for someone built like I appeared to be, though only one area of my body was actually hard. Hell, I was feeling a little emotionally erect...

I felt a sudden pleasant tugging on my swimming trunks as someone tried to slip them off my body and get to the rich, fertile area under them. Oh, and how I wanted to fertilize! I was ready to plant seeds all along the coast as far as the women would have me. I would be a virgin no more.

They had to be really careful with the suit, however. That certain area ready to fertilize wasn't exactly the most flexible at the moment, especially in the state of anticipation I was in.

Slowly, savoring the moment, I sat up to see which one of the women had finally grown bold enough to view my—

Jordan! I grabbed my trunks and yanked them back up as far as they would go, almost giving myself a wedgie, but the women in bikinis I had wanted so lustily to deflower held my arms down and then went for the legs. I couldn't move!

I looked back at Jordan in complete horror. He ever so gently began moving his hands up my legs, massaging them as he went. I tried frantically to get one of the girls to help me. They were mouthing words, but their voices didn't sound natural and what they said made no sense considering what was going on.

"I have an idea, Chester," one of them said. "Why don't we just be spontaneous and have Cheerios instead of corn flakes this morning?"

She spoke in my Aunt Virginia's voice.

"Well..." Another looked at me and sounded exactly like Uncle Chester. "...I don't think we should go so far out two days in a row, but why not?"

What did this very strange conversation have to do with what was going on?

I felt another tug on my swimsuit. Jordan was licking his lips and appeared more determined than ever to get the damn thing off me. I struggled to get a grip on the suit, but I couldn't move my hands because they were still being held down by the beach babes. No matter how hard I fought, they wouldn't let go, and Jordan was getting too damn close for comfort.

He finally had a solid grip on my trunks and gave them one hard yank as I tried to push my oppressors off me...

❧ ❧ ❧

Thud!

I opened my eyes and felt a dull ache along the entire right side of my body. The couch—I was no longer on the couch. Correction, I had launched myself *off* the couch. The struggle in my dream had also been acted out to some degree in real life. Actually, maybe this wasn't such a bad place to lie down for a while, especially since I had absolutely no desire to get up and I was too tired to care how comfortable I was.

Coming to California might have been my vacation, but it also symbolically meant giving up a great many things that made me comfortable in life—a bedroom, a bed, people who had a grasp of reality and, to some degree, heterosexuals. And what was with that dream? I had to be feeling stressed out for my subconscious to play games with me like that. Stressed out about what, though? My sexuality? That certainly wasn't worth stressing about. Hell, it was more like comic relief.

"Oh, good." Uncle Chester's voice interrupted the noise of the still-functioning grandfather clock. It was funny how I hadn't noticed it in a while. Now, if I could only drown *him* out. "Glad to see you rolled out of bed, Aaron. Heck of a landing, though. Just don't ever try out for the Olympics, unless it's the Special Olympics."

Well, wasn't he just witty?

"Virginia, why don't you get another cereal bowl down, and the young man can join us for breakfast before doing the dishes."

At least I understood why I'd heard their voices in my dream; it wouldn't take years of expensive therapy to figure that one out. Everything else might, but not that.

I sighed and began to untangle myself from the sheets. What time was it, anyway? I couldn't recall the last time I'd heard the clock go off, but it didn't seem like that much time had passed since I'd put my head down to sleep. A glance up at the damn thing informed me it was five minutes to seven.

This had to be some kind of sick joke! Nobody got up this early, nobody except...well, old people. It followed that only old people would think that having Cheerios instead of corn flakes for breakfast qualified as spontaneity. Maybe, if they were going to go all out, they'd try a bit of sugar or some fruit—after all, one is what one eats—with their flakes or Os, but I'd be willing to bet that didn't happen too often in this household.

I stumbled into the bathroom to brush my teeth while Aunt Virginia took two more bowls out of a cabinet and Uncle Chester knocked on Grandma's door. At least I wouldn't have to be miserable alone, though I'm sure Grandma had had a much better night's sleep than I did.

I sat down at the table and poured myself some cereal and milk. Grandma still hadn't appeared, so Uncle Chester went and pounded on her door again.

"Come on, Hotdog! The day is wasting!" he shouted. "Virginia and I have been up for forty-five minutes already. I've shaved, and we both showered, and breakfast is getting old. If you aren't out soon, it'll be time for lunch."

Oh, I was really enjoying this. I tended to be, for lack of a better word, a real bitch in the morning when I got up. I didn't care if it was for work or school or even if I slept in; I didn't want to see another living human being, let alone talk to one, for at least a solid half-hour. And happy? I didn't want see a happy person, either. That made everything so much worse for them in the end when I got a hold of them. Guaranteed, they weren't going to be happy when I finished with them.

My mother was the same way, so I can say I got it from her. However, she had to get it from someone, too, and that someone just happened to be my grandmother.

Speaking of whom, we could all hear the beast stirring and making her way over suitcases to the door she had so unceremoniously shut me out with last night. Uncle Chester looked over at me and grinned from ear to ear. He had no idea what was about to happen.

"Jesus Christ, Chester!" The door flew open, and there stood Grandma, makeup in worse shape than she'd gone to bed with, eyes dark and still almost completely shut, nostrils flaring and hair looking as though she'd stuck her finger in a light socket before coming out. Now I understood why she made sure to put her face on before joining the rest of humanity in the morning.

Uncle Chester gasped, and Aunt Virginia dropped her spoon.

"It's going on seven in the morning." Grandma dipped her words in anger and shot them out of her mouth like darts from a blowgun we used to imagine the naked women using in *National Geographic*. "Am I at work? No. Am I late for an appointment? No. Am I slightly hung over and in need of some rest? Yes!"

"Uh..." It was all Uncle Chester could say. I think he was still overwhelmed at the sight of his sister this early in the morning. Aunt Virginia was certainly horrified.

I, on the other hand, was only a little shocked and a great deal amused. The only thing going through my mind was "Go, Grandma!"

Uncle Chester must have seen the half-cockeyed grin on my face and decided to try and turn the tables.

"Well, I'm sorry there, Hotdog." He spoke soothingly and apologetically. I was immediately suspicious of his sudden change of attitude. "If you want to blame someone, you should be looking at that young man over there." He pointed at me, and I froze. "He's the one who said it was rude of you to miss breakfast, and for me to shout because you were a little hard of hearing."

"You've gotta be kidding me," I mumbled.

A few years ago, as the entire family sat down to eat Thanksgiving dinner, Grandma got everybody's attention and announced that we were going to say grace. As she started to do so, I shouted out the word "Grace" and made for the drumstick.

Nobody was really amused except for my father and me. My mother accused me later of trying to make too light of things in life, that not everybody was going to laugh and that not everything had to be funny. I never understood why that had to be true, when Murphy's Law had been screwing with my life for years.

Now it was Uncle Chester's Law, and I was the one who wasn't amused. I think I was starting to understand how frustrated Mable felt when I pulled all those pranks on her.

Grandma's head whipped around, an impressive close second to Linda Blair's complete head spin in *The Exorcist*, and glared at me. It looked as though she wanted to rip my head completely off my body with her bare hands but couldn't quite decide if that would hurt enough to get across her displeasure at being woken up so early. Instead, she stomped back into the bedroom and slammed the door shut behind her. I just thanked God she didn't have a loaded gun in her suitcase. The only thing generally ever loaded around Grandma was Grandma, unless there were relatives visiting or she was visiting them.

"Well." He shrugged. "I think she's a little upset. You best go use our shower, and then we'll get out of here before she comes back out. We have some shopping to do before company arrives."

I wondered what company he was talking about. It was probably more old people.

"Virginia will calm her down, and you can do the dishes after we get back."

Oh, well, that made my leaving with him to do some shopping okay, since I could do the dishes after we got back. I mean, that's what I was waiting to hear. Well, I was waiting to hear that and maybe an apology to Grandma followed by a confession about my innocence. That really would have been nice, but I doubted it would ever happen in this family and in this lifetime.

In fact, I would have been willing to bet money I didn't have that he had already convinced himself I really *had* told him those things. I'm sure his mind worked that way because I'd seen it in many of my relatives—namely, my aunts back home.

At this point, I needed a sign from God that the rest of this trip would get better. I had to stop saying that things couldn't get any worse because every time I did, inevitably, that's exactly what happened. Yes, a sign would be nice.

"Well, don't just stand there," Uncle Chester scolded. "You have running water in Michigan, don't you? I don't have to explain how a shower works, do I?"

Did he really want an answer?

"Skediddle!"

"Skedaddle," I corrected without even thinking about it.

"Don't start with me this morning, Arthur."

Aunt Virginia reemerged from the bedroom, and I took a change of clothes in with me along with my beach towel since neither of them had furnished me with a bath towel. I assumed that the guest towels were in the guest bathroom in the guest bedroom, which was now inhabited by a very pissed-off guest.

I stripped off my clothes once I was safely locked in the bathroom and laid them in a neat pile next to my clean ones. There was a Jacuzzi in the bathroom along with a shower stall. I ignored the tub and went for the stall. A shower was going to feel so good! Hell, I was willing to take a nice hot shower as the sign I was looking for.

I walked into the stall and turned the water on, adjusting it as I felt the temperature on my skin. Oh, it was heaven. The sweaty film and smell from the airplane washed off my body and down the drain, as did the smell of my sweat from the car ride to the party, the party itself and the conversation with and kiss from Jordan. All gone...Bye-bye...

Now, if only I could get rid of the memory of Jordan as easily as I did all of that.

I reached down for the soap and thought for a moment that I had gotten some water in my eye because it appeared that something had moved. However, the eye didn't feel irritated the way it generally did when water got into it. Then what the heck had I seen? Maybe I had just imagined a small black skittery object. Whatever...

I started lathering my arms and chest then moved down to my legs...which is when I saw the mutant spider. This thing had to be the amalgam of every spider I had ever killed in my entire life, and four times as large! It looked like it belonged inside one of those glass cases in a pet store instead of in a shower stall with me.

Maybe the shower wasn't the sign. Maybe the spider was. Well, if it died on the spot at the sight of me then that would be a good omen. If it didn't, and it moved, we'd have some severe problems.

"Shit...shit...shit..." I spoke softly so it wouldn't think I was shouting at it. "I can keep calm...not a problem. Just keep your calm, Marie and Donald's son..." I needed a plan to either escape or do the only sensible thing someone with arachnophobia could do: *kill it*!

My aim sucked, so flinging the bar of soap at it was no good. With my luck, the bar would just slip and slide around and eventually knock the damn spider right towards me. The little bottle of shampoo and conditioner I had with me would barely crush a fly, and I didn't want to get that close without knowing it would go crunch. I needed something else.

There was a medicine cabinet and sink just outside the shower, and I was sure it had lots of blunt heavy objects in it or on it. I took a step backwards towards the shower door, and the spider took a step forwards, as if anticipating what I was going to do. Keep calm. Think calm thoughts and remember above all else that it was a creature of

God. Treat it as such.

"Stay there, you little fucker!" Yeah, it was going to listen.

"Shit..." It was a face-off, its eight legs to my two and its numerous eyes to my two. I needed to show some bravery. I needed to stand up to my irrational fear and triumph in this battle. "You're going to die!" I sneered, and it started coming towards me at full speed. "Oh, shit!"

I flung the shower door open and took a flying leap out onto the floor that would have earned me a shot at being Bruce Willis's stunt double in *Die Hard*. Quickly, I searched the room for any object I could use to smash the little bastard and send it down the drain in little pieces.

"What's all that noise in there?" Uncle Chester's voice boomed out.

"I slipped," I shouted back.

"Well, you should get some more meat on those girly little bones of yours." I thought I heard him laughing. "Just be careful if you fall too close to the drain. I don't want to have to call a plumber if you slide down and clog it up."

I wanted to clog his breathing hole, that's what I wanted to do. First, however, I had to kill a spider.

I finally saw something I could use—a can of vanilla-scented air freshener. One of my relatives obviously had a problem with unsavory scents. I grabbed it and located my nemesis, which was trying to make its way up the wall to get a better jump at my face. Not today you won't. Not ever!

It didn't take much effort to aim, considering how big the damn thing was.

Crunch!

It felt so good to do—and very therapeutic—so I decided to live in the moment.

Crunchcrunchcrunchcrunchcrunchcrunchcrunch crunch!

Also therapeutic was going to be my leaving the remains under Uncle Chester's pillow for him to find tonight when he went to bed.

I carefully peeled the can off the wall and tried to make sure that as much of the spider remain intact or in a lump as I could. After cleaning the bottom of the can off and replacing it back on the toilet, I dried my hands and carefully wrapped the remains on a piece of toilet paper. It would safely stay there for the remainder of the shower and until I was sure I wouldn't be seen putting it where I intended.

This entire procedure didn't take very long, and I was enjoying my shower within a minute or two. That didn't last very long, either, though, because I was also racing against Grandma, and I knew she'd be looking for me.

❧ ❧ ❧

"You seem pretty excited there, Alvin," Uncle Chester commented and gave me a quick look before turning his attention back to the traffic in front of him. "I imagine you don't get too much company out there in Michigan."

"You got that right," I agreed. Little did he know just exactly what I was excited about, although he'd sure-enough find out tonight.

Closing their bedroom door to finish getting dressed didn't arouse suspicion, nor was figuring out which side of the bed was his. There was no real proof that I was the culprit, and I would never admit it. Hey, I did have some of my family traits in me, after all! It would be logical for him to

114

assume he crushed the damn spider either when he laid his head down on the pillow or put his hand underneath it. Either way, he'd be getting one hell of a surprise tonight.

In the meantime, it was back to his comment about us not getting much company back in Michigan.

"Once in a while, a man travels through our village with his cart and sharpens our knives or sells us some new copper pots and pans." I paused dramatically. "If we're really lucky, we even hear news from some of the other villages."

Uncle Chester eyed me curiously. Either he was considering the level of my sarcasm and general smartass nature, or he was recalling his own childhood, before the invention of motorized cars. I'd be willing to bet that Michael Crichton went to him for information and cross-referencing about dinosaurs when *Jurassic Park* was being written.

I really shouldn't have been so cruel as to think thoughts like that after what I'd done. Yes, the man who was technically my great-uncle, but whom I simply called uncle, was annoying, yet I had to give him some credit. He hadn't embarrassed me in public. It was only in front of my relatives, and I think that was considered acceptable in certain foreign cultures.

Things couldn't get any worse, but they could be maintained the way they were or get better. For one, we were having company later on and that had potential. I really needed to be optimistic.

We pulled into the parking lot of some super-market called Ralph's. There weren't many other people there that early, with the exception of the staff and a few other elderly shoppers. Uncle Chester pulled a handwritten list out of his pocket as we walked through the doors and scanned it. A few employees were hanging around the aisle closest to us and talking to someone I assumed was their supervisor or the store manager. They were basically being given a pep talk about making a greater contribution to the store by doing their job to the best of their abilities.

That gave me an idea. I felt it would be a positive gesture on my part if I offered to go pick out some chips and other snacks and then pay for them as my contribution to the lunch and dinner Chester was providing, and stated as much.

"Why, that's a fine idea, Albert!" he exclaimed rather loudly, catching the attention of the employees and supervisor. "Why don't you go see what you can find, and I'll catch up with you in a few minutes."

I started to walk away feeling like we had really reached some kind of truce when he called back after me, "Just don't let me catch you shoplifting again because I won't be bailing you out of jail this time."

"Son of a..." I turned around, but he was already gone in search of the items on his list. The staff people standing close by were looking at me with expressions that told me they didn't know what to expect. Was it true or wasn't it? I shook my head and faced them. "He was joking."

To try and explain any further would only make the situation worse, but I decided to try.

"He's senile."

It only got worse.

I went to search for some chips and pretzels, and there was always one of them close by. At least they took turns to try and make it look a little less obvious. I appreciated that and held my head high, as if nothing was wrong or going on. Maybe I had been too nice to him. Maybe I would have to go down to his level just to make him understand that I didn't want to be messed with anymore. Maybe...

"Did you get everything you wanted?" Uncle Chester asked me when I joined him at the checkouts. I nodded and got my wallet out. "You really don't have to do this, you know. I figured you'd make it up to us when we take Hotdog to Disneyland."

"Disneyland?" They were taking Grandma to Disneyland? Nothing was mentioned about that before I left home, and it seemed obvious I wasn't invited, so how, exactly, was I going to make my meals up to them if I wasn't going? "What, exactly, did you have in mind for me to do while you were all off yanking Mickey's mouse?"

"Well..." He paused. "...you recall those dirt piles in front of the house?" I did. "They're quite an eyesore and could really stand to be moved down the block at one of the houses that's still being built. It shouldn't take more than a day."

That, apparently, made all the difference in the world to him. The only thing it did for me was increase my desire to commit a felony or somehow escape. Even spending an uncertain week with Jordan was starting to sound better than this. At least there I'd know where I stood and where I was expected to lie—like that would happen anyway.

I wasn't afraid of work like doing dishes or even

moving dirt, but I did resent why I was doing them. This really had nothing to do with earning my way through my vacation at all. It was because I was young, should be seen and not heard, couldn't understand complex issues in life like how to pack suitcases in a car or how to operate an air conditioner, and that was simply the way Uncle Chester's reality existed. All of this somehow got by me in life, at least in his eyes. It wouldn't matter if I was already out of college and making millions of dollars, because then I would just be part of that "corrupt capitalist system" and therefore part of the problem. No one could know better than he did, and that put me in a no-win situation.

Except, I don't like no-win situations.

If I stayed with him, that would mean I'd probably never get out to the beach, and *that* meant losing my chances of giving myself up to the bikini vixens. I couldn't have that.

※ ※ ※

Uncle Chester immediately started preparing the backyard to entertain guests when we got back. Grandma didn't say a word to me, though she looked a great deal better after her shower and recently applied new face. At least it wasn't running into other areas of itself anymore.

Instead, she took out some tablecloths and stacks of plastic silverware and paper plates and began to organize all of that. I, in the meantime, started on the dishes.

As I was stacking everything into piles of what I wanted to wash first to last, Aunt Virginia came out of her bedroom with something in her hand and wearing a hairnet over curlers in her hair. With the

118

other two pains-in-my-ass outside, this seemed the perfect opportunity to speak with her. Of all the relatives I'd met, she seemed to have the best head on her shoulders, or at least the quietest one.

Actually, it was her silence that led me to believe she might be very nonjudgmental, and I really needed to talk to somebody right now with that quality.

"Just getting started," I told her and held up a plate. She gazed at me ever so meekly and nodded. "I was really hoping I'd get a chance to talk to you."

I turned back around and started filling up the sink with water and soap.

"Last night was kind of hectic, and I didn't want you getting the wrong idea about me. That whole bit with me pretending to pound on Grandma's door...it, uh, wasn't what it looked like." I paused and chuckled at what I must have looked like. "To tell you the truth, this vacation isn't exactly turning out like I thought it would." I took another glance her way to be sure she was listening and not in the process of leaving the room and saw that she was sitting at the kitchen table.

"I shouldn't be saying this to you at all, and I mean no disrespect to you as a hostess," I continued, "but this vacation has been completely fu—screwed up. Nobody told me what to expect, and quite honestly, I was really looking forward to this." I started with the glasses. "Things aren't really so complicated back home, but sometimes you need a break from everything that goes on to actually be able to see that. Sometimes, we get set in a pattern or way of living that we don't know how to break. In the end, it doesn't allow us to expand and grow as people. If anybody really needs to grow, it's probably me."

Was I being too harsh on myself? One thing was for sure—Aunt Virginia was really easy to talk to.

"This may sound silly, but I'm not very good at relating to women my age. I don't understand them very well. Actually..." I chuckled. "...I'm not very good at relating to people at *any* age. Heck, just last night I tried talking to this one guy who was at the party and he ended up..."

I caught myself just in time!

"Let's not go where that one went. Suffice to say, it was confusing, at best.

"Anyway, I think it helps—really helps—to talk about this stuff because then I don't feel like I'm feeling sorry for myself."

Aunt Virginia was being a very good sport about listening to me babble. Talking to her was really a pleasure because she listened.

"Nobody wants to listen to anybody anymore. They aren't like you. I mean, Uncle Chester certainly wouldn't let me talk to him about anything other than how my life is going to serve him during my stay here."

He was damn frustrating, but how could I say that to her tactfully?

"I'm sure he's a good man, especially to you. The two of you have a new home, I don't see any bruises on you at all, and I haven't heard you complain, so he must be doing something right and that's great." I really was happy for her. "Unless he cut out your tongue, which would explain why I never hear you talk, but that's beside the point.

"I really want this trip to be special. Actually, I

was kind of hoping that I would *meet* someone special."

Flashes of the previous night with Jordan came readily to mind and seemed to be invading my waking thoughts on a regular basis, but he wasn't who I wanted to be with. I wanted to mate with the women on the beach, which brought back the memory of the dream and its very bizarre twist.

"Unfortunately, it hasn't happened yet, but I'm hopeful." I finished the few bowls and spoons that were left next to the sink. "Sometimes I have to wonder if my problem is just me or if I'm meeting the wrong women. Am I really that bad?"

She remained respectfully quiet, letting me sort it out for myself.

"Am I really worth knowing?" I was fishing for a response this time. "Or am I just being too hard on myself here?"

Nothing. *You can jump in here at any time!* "If I can find someone who listens to me even half as much as you do, then I'll consider myself lucky." I turned and faced her. "What do you think?"

"What?" Aunt Virginia looked up at me and removed her hair net along with a tiny pair of earphones that were connected to a Walkman sitting on her lap. That must have been the object in her hand, and she apparently hadn't realized I'd been talking to her the entire time. "Did you cut yourself, dear? Chester said you had sensitive skin...or did he say you were the sensitive type?" She thought about it for a moment. "I don't remember. In any case, did you need something?"

"No," I replied, "nothing at all."

❧ ❧ ❧

121

The guests turned out to be Uncle Chester's son Kenny, his wife Jenny and their two boys, Benny, age nine, and Lenny, age seven. Yes, I thought it was a joke at first, too.

Jenny and I started talking almost right away and didn't stop until it was time to eat. By then, I had updated her on how the trip was going, that I had hoped to see the beaches and experience a little bit of what living in California was all about and what Uncle Chester's ultimate plans for me were if I stayed there. She was appalled—literally appalled—that I hadn't started drinking anything stronger than Pepsi before they'd arrived and only slightly surprised at the conditions of my stay. She was definitely family, all right.

We caught a glimpse of a list Uncle Chester had been making of all the things he wanted me to accomplish around the house during my time there. Jenny took Kenny aside before the end of the evening, and the two of them plotted my escape. I didn't know yet if it was really to help me or to put a wrench in the man's plans, but during a lull in the conversation, she helped me get my suitcase out to their minivan unnoticed. Did I care if it was to help me or hinder Uncle Chester? Not really, because, undoubtedly, both would be accomplished.

Jenny also told me not to worry about what to tell my hosts about my leaving. She had something in mind and felt confident there wouldn't be any problems.

Just before leaving, she suggested out loud to Kenny that they take me for a ride and show me some of the sights that were spectacular to look at during the night hours.

"Oh, Kenny," Uncle Chester immediately objected, "you don't need to put yourself out for the boy. He's perfectly happy right where he's at."

"We have two children," Jenny chimed in before her husband could reply, "so I don't think 'putting out' is a problem for us."

I chuckled at her smartass comment and received a dirty look from Grandma. Jenny was like the relative I never knew I had but would have wanted if I knew I did!

"Besides, if the kid stays here, he'll be lucky if you take the handcuffs and shackles off of him long enough for him to get a decent tan." She looked at me and winked. "And in case you hadn't heard, slavery is so passé. It was also outlawed some time ago...probably when you were in your late teens."

Ooohhh...That had to hurt.

Jenny reminded me of Sally Field at this point, because I liked her! I really liked her! This woman had to be good to have broken the male ego of one of our family members, especially the crown prince's. Anyone who could do that would undoubtedly have little difficulty in standing up to the king, much like she had just done. Guess I knew who wore the panties in *that* family.

Besides, if Uncle Chester thought I was going to pass up an opportunity like this, he was nuts! Jenny had already promised to take me to a number of the beaches and introduce me to something called Corona. I didn't know if that was a new kind of condom or aphrodisiac, but as long as I was safe and spawning, I really didn't care.

"I don't know about this," Grandma said. "Marie and Donald entrusted me with his safety, and I don't think they'd like him running off like this and taking advantage of you." She looked over at me and frowned. "I think Chester is right. What's-his-face is fine here where we can keep an eye on him."

"Uh, excuse me," I finally broke in. "What's-his-face—I mean me—is nineteen years old and a legal adult, so I think he can make his own executive decisions."

Uncle Chester and Grandma were peering at me, unable to comprehend why I was opening my mouth and speaking when I hadn't been properly invited to do so.

"I understand and appreciate Grandma's feelings of responsibility, but there is a much deeper issue involved here." I seemed to have all their attention now. "I want very much to be a writer, and that means getting out and experiencing life. Now, while I appreciate the offer to experience white slavery firsthand, I think I'm going to pass and go for the real essence of life here in California— Corona and beach babes." My search for love in California was officially on!

Kenny, Jenny, Benny, Lenny and I left the house that night with an understanding with the elders that we were officially agreeing we were dis-agreeing. Uncle Chester and Grandma never gave up trying to change my mind, often using words like *duty* and *family* as a part of their argument. It was as if I should somehow be feeling challenged to do a certain amount of hard labor at Uncle Chester's before going back to Michigan to the job that awaited me and the classes at school that would follow shortly thereafter. Funny thing is, I didn't feel challenged, not at all. I felt Uncle

Chester was challenged, though.

"I'm very disappointed in you," Grandma said sternly and peered at me with disapproval.

"I'm crushed." I reached over and planted a quick kiss on her cheek. When I turned around, Uncle Chester was blocking my way into the van.

"You're not showing a great deal of maturity, young man." He spoke slowly, and as if it were some kind of warning that bad things were going to happen if I left.

"Uncle Chester." I looked him right in the eyes and tried my best to look defeated. I couldn't believe he had actually told me I wasn't showing a great deal of maturity when he had felt it was perfectly acceptable to inform store employees I had been caught and jailed for shoplifting in the past. What could I say to a man who did that? "Bite me."

I grabbed his hand, shook it and squeezed past him into the vehicle.

We were roaring out of the subdivision moments later and heading towards the freeway and freedom. I wondered what sights they would show me, especially since it was already getting a bit late for their children. The boys looked as tired as I felt.

It was only eleven, but back home it was two a.m.; and that made all the difference in the world. I needed to get some sleep so I would be ready and fertile for my first romp with a beach babe. Actually, I really didn't want to be fertile with one as much as I just wanted to have sex with one or two or three of them...maybe more. They would be all I needed to get Jordan out of my mind, especially since I'd just bothered to acknowledge he was still in there.

That was a strange thought. Was it that important to me to get him out of my mind, or was there something else? I'd often wondered why so many people were doing things I wanted to but never did because I knew they were wrong. What made me so moralistic? What was I trying to prove by not having sex? I didn't do it in high school because I freaked, but why did I freak? I'd been close to love, but I didn't commit sexually. Why?

Sex would have been so easy, yet it had never felt right. Part of me wanted someone special and another part of me just wanted someone. What would I be proving if I did have sex?

Maybe, if I just got the sex part out of the way, I would be able to concentrate on the more meaningful aspects of relationships. How did Jordan feel about matters like this?

Well, there he was again.

Admittedly, if I was gay, I could have done a lot worse than Jordan, at least based entirely on looks. I had no idea what kind of a person he was on the inside, however. Hell, he could have been telling me what he thought I wanted to hear just so he could score. The thought of him wanting to score didn't make me laugh, but the fact he tried to score with me did. I mean, this guy lived in California with movie stars and studs on steroids on the beach, so why me? What was the attraction? Maybe he just liked virgins.

Oh, God, did I make it that obvious to him that I was a virgin? Did any of this really matter? No. Okay, then, concentrate on the vixens, the tigresses, she-lions, daughters of joy, mistresses, concubines, temptresses, nymphomaniacs, hystero-maniacs, uteromaniacs and clitoromaniacs...

"Andy." Jenny turned around in the front seat to look at me. "We're almost there." She broke out into a huge grin. "You're going to love the Ambassador!"

"Great." The Ambassador? Wasn't that the name of the bridge some of my friends and I took going over to Canada?

It must be a fairly common name to use in states where bridges were an actual attraction. It wasn't like tourists would find a large structure like that in Wisconsin, where all those people had going for them was cheese. Here, the bridges had to have a grand or extravagant name.

"What's the Ambassador?"

6

An incredible light filled my eyes, and I thought for sure that I was on fire, mostly because of the amount of pain it caused me. My voice wouldn't work very well when I tried to speak and what did come out was a combination of unintelligible sounds. Why was it so difficult to remember where I was and what had happened to me?

I felt something on top of me, but I couldn't tell what it was. Ironically, there was no noise. Fires made noise, didn't they? Either I'd gone deaf, too, or I wasn't really on fire. Very curious.

I think I was lying down, my head was definitely killing me, the light was too damn bright and my body felt like it had been hit by a large truck that had been speeding far faster than it should have down an LA freeway.

Where in the hell was I, and what had happened to me? Maybe I was in a hospital and feeling the after-effects of some accident we'd gotten into. The fire may have been real then, but I'd lived and my mind was blocking out the scene to save me from more trauma.

I must have been pretty scarred and burned on my head to feel the way I did. Maybe I'd need plastic surgery. I've always been told by my peers that I should have it anyway, so now I had an excuse to have it done. Who could I ask to look like?

My stomach grumbled quite loudly, and I almost doubled over in pain. The damn muscles in that area felt like they were completely shot. It did, however, force me to open my eyes.

I was in a bedroom—a normal bedroom, not some hospital room. The thing I felt on top of me was a large blanket, and the light was sunlight coming in between the blinds on a nearby window. I was getting it full in the face because I was on the top of a bunk bed.

A quick glance around turned up very little. I was alone, and my suitcase was on the floor beside the bed. Also, in becoming conscious, I noticed an extremely foul stench that I soon realized was my breath. Whatever had happened, I never bothered to brush my teeth before going to bed.

I hadn't bothered to undress, either. *God, what I must look like.*

The scent of freshly cooked bacon reached my nostrils, and my stomach growled again. The combination of hunger and light was what probably roused me from my sleep, something I almost dismissed as the slumber of the damned compliments of my imagination. What was I missing, here, other than my memory?

Actually, memory was pretty much it.

Curious as to what sudden turn my life had taken, I opened the bedroom door, made my way down a long hallway and finally emerged in the kitchen. Jenny was cooking at the stove; she sensed my presence and turned to greet me.

"Well, good morning!" She appeared far too perky for my taste. "You look like you could use a shower."

That had to be the understatement of the year. I was just glad I hadn't woken up in some stranger's house or in a hotel room next to a dead body. Nah, that only happened in the movies.

"What happened last night?" It was the only thing I could think to ask, mostly because it would clear everything up. At least, I hoped it would.

"Kenny and I thought you might not remember." She chuckled as she spoke. "We dropped the kids off here with the babysitter and then took off for the Ambassador."

"I don't remember that at all." I searched my memory as hard as I could, but it was all a haze. I didn't even remember them telling me they were going to drop the kids off let alone actually doing it. "Did I drink or something?" I shouldn't have been able to since I'm underage.

"Oh, yeah." Jenny suddenly looked guilty. "But that's kind of our fault. We know the people who work there and told them you were with us, so they served you. You started with a few Coronas and then someone from another table sent over two shots of Jungle Juice. At that point, you weren't exactly thinking too clearly, but you were really enjoying yourself!" She savored the memory. "Three shots of tequila, two spontaneous karaoke songs and one limbo contest later, you passed out."

I was mortified.

"Kenny and I had to help carry you out to the car, and you kept saying some very odd things the entire way. You were laughing, pointing to the sky and saying 'I see them! I see the dolphins! Alphaville was right!'"

I was *completely* mortified.

"Please tell me that's all I said and did." Maybe Uncle Chester and Grandma had been right in thinking I shouldn't have left, but for very different reasons. I sang karaoke? I performed in a limbo contest? I talked about Alphaville and dolphins. I *would* have to bring up music when I was trashed. That was okay as long as I didn't go any further and bring up Samantha Fox and her tits! That was where I drew the line.

"Well, there were two other things." Jenny blushed a bit. "We got the impression you were rather fond of Samantha Fox's breasts."

Shit!

"By 'we,' you mean you and Kenny?" Things could have been worse. I could have told my great-aunt and uncle. Damage control was at work here.

"Actually..." She looked back down at what she was cooking, obviously trying to save me some amount of embarrassment. "...me, Kenny and everyone else in the bar. You kind of announced it while doing a karaoke striptease tribute to 'Touch Me (I Want Your Body).'"

"Oh, God." I didn't feel so good. Maybe it was best that I didn't remember anything that had happened. I might have wanted to take more than just a few aspirins to end the pain. Maybe a bottle or two...

How in the hell could I explain my actions? I

couldn't. What if my parents found out? What if *Grandma* found out? She'd personally haul my ass right back to Michigan and tell my parents exactly what I was doing out here. Within forty-eight hours, I'd gotten drunk, been kissed by a man, pissed my grandmother and great-uncle off, gotten drunk again, performed a striptease at a bar I couldn't remember doing the following morning. I think I was catching up to my peers back at the university with sufficient speed.

"Oh, don't be so upset." Jenny flashed me a look that suggested there was something else I wasn't being told. "They loved it! Hell, they gave you a standing ovation..."

What? She'd stopped in mid-sentence. There was definitely something being left out here. What was it?

"And that's when I passed out?" I hoped.

"No, that's when you did your encore and sang 'Boom Boom (Let's Go Back To My Room).'"

"And your telling me this is supposed to make me feel better how?"

"Like I said, don't worry about it." She finished with whatever she was making—pancakes, it smelled like—and put them in the oven to stay warm. "They loved what you did. In fact, I think three or four people offered to take you back home with them so you could sleep it off."

That sounded promising.

"Young women with bodacious ta-tas looking for a meaningful relationship with Mr. Right?"

"No." Jenny gave me a strange look. "More like older men looking to play sugar daddy with Mr. Right Now, who happens to have a youthful face and tight ass."

"Sugar what?" Wasn't a sugar daddy a candy bar? I definitely wasn't up on all of this California lingo. "What made them think I had a tight ass?"

"Please." She rolled her eyes. "Everybody saw your ass. Believe me, it's tight."

"I don't think I want to hear anymore." I didn't want to be a pop star. I only wanted to be a writer, and singing wasn't a requirement, let alone drunken singing. The last time I'd done that was at Cedar Point in the little recording studio there. Soberly listening to me drunkenly singing Robert Palmer's "Addicted To Love" had convinced me never to do that again. Well, until now.

"My nephew helped us get you into the house, and he was the one who put you to bed." Jenny shook her head again and chuckled. "You must watch a lot of horror movies or something because you kept referring to him as the 'son of Satan' and insisted that Kenny and I search his scalp for a scar in the shape of six-sixty-six then sacrifice him so the world could live. It gave us quite a laugh."

"It seems I live to amuse lately." I was completely exasperated.

Whoever her nephew was, I hoped he hadn't felt insulted. I also hoped he didn't believe in going by first impressions alone. Jenny or Kenny would have explained the situation to him, and the fact I was from out-of-state would surely add to his understanding of my behavior and stupidity.

"I'm going to go take my shower." I turned to leave.

"That's fine," she assured me. "I put a towel and washcloth in the bathroom for you and...oh, listen."

She stopped me in my tracks. "I have to take the boys to baseball practice shortly, so the J-man will finish getting breakfast ready. You can eat with him, and then when we get back later on, we'll talk about where we can go while you're here." She smiled warmly.

"I appreciate all this," I told her sincerely. "Thank you."

"You're welcome." She picked up her purse and called for the boys. "We'll see you in a bit."

I went back to the bedroom and opened my suitcase for all the things I was going to need. The first goal I had was to brush my teeth, then shave and finally shower. It was probably a good thing the kids hadn't seen me this morning looking like I did. They could see me later when I looked semi-quasi-normal. Somehow, though, I would have thought Jenny and Kenny would have enrolled them in a wine-tasting class instead of Little League. Actually, they probably did.

Drinking seemed to be a sport on this side of the family, and I could only assume they all started at a young age. I could never do it, mostly because I didn't have much of a tolerance. After last night, I didn't even want to think about drinking again, so I really didn't need to bother with working up a tolerance.

The shower felt wonderful! Combined with a fresh shave and the taste of toothpaste still in my mouth, I felt like a new...person in my late teens.

Hopefully this "J-man" nephew of Jenny's hadn't eaten all the bacon I'd smelled earlier. Despite however much I'd drunk the previous night, I needed food. The pancakes smelled pretty good, too, and I think I knew why. There was the smallest hint of vanilla mixed in with the scent, and I loved pancakes with a bit of that in them. So, my cousin was a gourmet. It sure beat corn flakes or Special K or Cheerios at my great-aunt and uncle's place.

I finished dressing, did something funky with my hair then put all of my crap back into the suitcase. Someone—I suspected the J-man—could be heard setting out plates on the table. It was time I met this...what was he, anyway? A second or third cousin by marriage? Whatever. It was time I met him.

"Good morning." I tried to sound as perky and good-natured as I possibly could to make up for the previous night. What I saw staring back at me made my entire life flash before my eyes...or at least events from the previous thirty-six hours. "Son of a bitch..."

"Good morning! You *could* just call me by my real name, although son of a bitch is a bit kinder than son of Satan."

"Jordan..." I spoke the name just to make sure I wasn't still dreaming. "You're the J-man?"

He turned and faced me as if there could be no other.

"And you put me to bed last night?" The mere thought of that made me want to go and take another shower. Not really, but I should have been thinking that. After all, it would be a normal reaction, right?

"Yeah, I put you to bed...even put you on the top bunk," he informed me and then appeared to be in deep thought. "I always figured you for a top."

"A top what?" That I struck him as someone used

135

to taking the top bunk was eerie, mostly because it was correct. I liked the top. I was used to the top. However, it really had nothing to do with anything.

"*You* know." He put his hands in front of him, one on top of the other, then rubbed them together. I think I cringed a bit when I finally realized he was referring to sex, but he only raised an eyebrow and smirked at my discomfort.

"Don't go there," I warned him.

"Oh, take it easy." Jordan opened up the oven and took out a plate of pancakes. "I didn't even peek."

I relaxed a little.

"Well, maybe for a moment."

I tensed back up, and he laughed out loud, his way of telling me he was only joking. At least, he better have been joking.

"After all the stuff I heard you were mumbling on the way home from the bar, I was just glad my aunt and uncle didn't hear the stuff you were saying to me last night while I was trying to get you into bed."

"Oh, please."

I had to expect this from him. Now he would try to tell me I had confessed parts of my life to him that he had suspected all along and that I needed him to be my teacher in this new and trying period of my life. Fat bloody chance! How many other people had he done this to? How many times had that been said to him before he caught on to how well it worked as an easy way to get sex?

"Get a life." I sat down at the table and grabbed a few pieces of bacon. Thank God there were some left.

"You don't believe me?" he asked playfully.

"I believe you're full of shit. Care to prove me wrong?"

He couldn't, and we both knew it. Again, that was what I was supposed to be thinking. After doing a striptease karaoke tribute, an encore, limbo contest and babbling about dolphins in the sky—hell, anything was possible. For all I knew, I told him the recipe for a baked potato.

Still, I needed to reassure my own ego. "You can't, can you?" I started taking some pancakes and considered telling him to eat my blueberries. It sounded too cliché, though.

"Well." Jordan scratched his chin. "I understand that you've been having some dreams where you've got trouble keeping your swimming trunks up around me."

I hacked up a small piece of bacon that had suddenly lodged itself in the back of my throat. Nuts! He wasn't joking after all. Why couldn't I have been conscious during all this? I could have either changed the story a bit or just kept my damn mouth shut, but now there was no telling exactly how much of that story and dream he knew. Well, he knew enough, and that was way too much for my comfort.

Jordan was right about one point—it was a damn good thing my cousins weren't around to hear this exchange. I wondered if they knew about him, what he was.

"Are you okay?" He was staring at me with an expression of concern.

"I'm fine," I said at last. "I'm just busy hating you right now."

"You really are homophobic." Jordan frowned.

"Would you please stop calling me that?"

"It's the first time I've called you that." Something dawned on him. "Do you even know what that means?"

I shook my head. It obviously didn't mean what I thought it did, and whatever it was sounded like a serious matter. This was really strange. I'd been correcting Uncle Chester like crazy, and all that intelligence was just gone every time I was around Jordan. He was obviously bad for me.

"It means you hate gay people."

"I don't hate gay people." Of all the people I'd known in my life and disliked, even hated, it never occurred to me to hate someone specifically because they were gay. Maybe I avoided them more so than others, but I don't think I hated them. I don't even think I hated Jordan, not really. He was just a convenient target for me to take my aggressions out on, but I didn't want to hurt him.

I also think that he and I were a lot alike in that we enjoyed pushing limits and had unusual senses of humor, but that was where it ended.

"And I don't hate you."

"Sure you do." A spark appeared in his eye. "And they say that those who hate gays the most are usually the ones hiding their own repressed desires. That's why they hate them...because they're reminded of what they might really be." He was definitely pushing the limits of my temper.

"The only desire I'm repressing now is to kick your ass."

"*My* ass?" Jordan scoffed. "Seems to me that everybody's talking about *your* ass."

"Shut up!" I gave him a dirty look. "Nobody is talking about my ass." How long had my cousin been gone? Shouldn't she be back sometime soon, and didn't Jordan have a job he needed to get to? Didn't he have a life, or did he feel he was making up for it by torturing me?

"You know..." A mischievous look I'd seen at the anniversary party appeared once more on his face. "...you're really argumentative and aggressive."

"I am not," I insisted. "Fuck off!"

He grew quiet for a moment, probably enjoying the fact he'd won that little verbal bout. I'd been so worked up that I completely neglected to pay attention to how he was setting me up. That would be the last time I gave him that advantage.

Of all the people there were in the world, I couldn't believe this joker was my cousin. What had I done to deserve this? Who had I pissed off in life that I should be paid back with him? Meeting him once and then having him show up in a dream was bad enough, but to have to endure his company for the rest of the trip...

That was it. I was going to call Uncle Chester up, apologize, grovel, whatever it took, and go back there.

"My aunt said you might enjoy going out to the beach this afternoon and then doing some shopping at Tower Records later in the evening. Ever been there? It's the largest record store in the world."

Okay, maybe I'd go back later tonight or even real early tomorrow morning. I'd at least give it until then. Besides, Jordan was suddenly being nice, which made me both relieved and suspicious. At least he wasn't making sexual innuendoes anymore. That was a definite plus.

"Am I to understand you'll be going with us?" I might as well find out now.

"Uh…yeah." He looked as if I had just insulted him again. "You don't want me to?"

"I just wondered if you had a job or something to go to…a home of your own maybe, or with parents, some brothers or sisters…a life outside this sphere of my immediate existence." I paused. No matter how hard I tried, I just couldn't stand being nice to him, and I didn't know why. It was as if I was afraid of him, afraid to let him see a certain side of me, a likeable side. I had opened up to him a bit during the party and the results were…unexpected.

Before that, however, he had opened up a bit, too, and I'd heard things that, for research purposes only, I would have liked to hear him expand on. Asking questions, though, might give him the wrong impression, and I had to keep that distance between us perfectly clear at all times.

"Let's see," Jordan began, "my summer job just ended, and the reason I don't have another one is because I'm still working on my degree and classes start pretty soon. As for parents, yes, I have some, but I left home the day I turned eighteen. From there, it was a matter of going from one dead end job to another just to make enough money to rent a room somewhere and eat an occasional meal. When Aunt Jenny found out, she and Ken took me in and helped me do what I needed to start taking classes and get this intellect of mine educated." He paused for a breath. "I may not have had the easiest life in the world, but it hasn't been the most difficult, either, which is why you won't hear me complain.

Any other questions or comments?"

"You mean now that you've made me feel like a total jackass?" I looked right at him. "Nothing really comes to mind." A few moments of silence passed.

"It's amazing what happens when you begin to understand that there's more to a person than you first saw or thought, isn't it?" Jordan eyed me evenly. "A lot of people believe ignorance is bliss." He shook his head. "But ignorance is just that—ignorance. We have to choose how much we really want to know before passing any kind of judgment."

He stood up from the table then and left me alone to finish my breakfast. I hated to admit it, but he had a point. It seemed everybody did lately, except me.

⚜ ⚜ ⚜

Luckily, I didn't have to wait very long for Jenny to come back. One of her kids was suspected of adding yellow food coloring to a cooler of water and telling everyone, including the parents, that they were drinking urine. It seemed no one was amused, least of all the adults.

I think that only a boy would come up with something like that, and only a mother would react like an escaped mental patient about it. Fathers would chastise the child, perhaps escort them home and even ground them if the prank was severe enough. Mothers, however, had an entirely different approach. They dealt with pranks the way Martha Stewart chastised her illegal immigrant workers—loudly, in a foreign language and with lots of obscenities.

Jenny turned out to be one of those feminist mothers who wasn't afraid to punish the children without first consulting her husband. While it wasn't unusual for the kids not to be able to appeal a ruling by their mother, it was unusual that the husband couldn't. Jenny and Kenny must have had an unspoken understanding between them that she laid down the law and he followed it. Unfortunately, that meant someone now had to stay home with the boys, since one of them was grounded and the youngest would only be bored going out with us.

Jordan volunteered to remain behind so we could go. I wondered if he did it because of the exchange between us earlier. That was really a stupid thought. Of course that was why he didn't come, and I doubted I could have been much ruder to him. Didn't people like him get used to that, though? Didn't they know that by broadcasting something like homosexuality they would be practically advertising for trouble?

In light of that, it seemed rather pointless to embrace such a choice and go against the majority of society. No, it actually seemed more ignorant and self-destructive than anything else. Why would he do that to himself? Why would anybody?

"Let's get outta here!" Jenny yelled after we changed into our swimsuits, grabbed some towels and headed for the door. We pulled into a driveway a short time later, and another woman ran out to greet us. She had short dark hair, wore a swimsuit that truly complimented her body and carried a rather large bag.

"Diane," Jenny introduced us as the woman got into the minivan, "this is my cousin from Michigan, Andy. He's a writer, so I wouldn't piss him off because he'll write about you."

Both women laughed. Apparently, this was funny to them. My parents were extremely supportive of what direction I wanted to go in life, and I doubt very much they would have laughed at that joke. My writing about them was exactly what my mother was hoping to avoid!

"A writer, huh?" Diane looked me over while Jenny backed out and headed for the open road. It was rather a relief to see that someone of the opposite sex was looking at me in that way instead of Jordan. I certainly felt a bit more comfortable, if not also more aware of my posture and lack of a physique. "Have you considered transferring out to UCLA? I think I heard that they have a really great writing program there, especially if it has anything to do with screenwriting. It's the perfect area for it."

"Yeah...true. It's convenient with the university and Hollywood being so close together, but I'm not sure screenwriting is what I want to do yet." Actually, I didn't know what the hell I wanted to do yet other than just wanting to write. Write what, though? Here was another great moment in my life with no focus. "So, I guess probably not."

"Jenny's nephew Jordan goes to UCLA," She informed me.

"Then definitely not."

Diane gave me a puzzled look, but I ignored it. I wondered if she knew about him.

"Besides, the school I'm going to now shows some promise, and I really hate to cut anything short there without seeing if I've the potential for writing or for becoming...a garbage collector." I made a face that reflected my thoughts on having that as my future occupation.

"My husband's a garbage collector." She spoke matter-of-factly.

"Uh...hmm. There's certainly...nothing wrong with that at all." I was going to crash and burn quickly if I didn't come up with a save. It was a good thing Uncle Chester wasn't here to tell her how prejudiced I was against farmers and ditchdiggers, too. "It just isn't writing, which is what I seem to have a passion for. Heck, there's money to be made from garbage collecting." I tried to sound positive and sincere. "It's an honest job, not like having to sell your body in some cheap strip club while taking clients in the back for a quickie and hoping that the tips cover the grocery bill for the next week."

"Actually, Andy," Jenny gave me a side look, "Diane's sister is an exotic dancer in a strip club in Seattle, and she has to hope that her tips cover the cost of raising her four children and the grocery bill."

"Right..." Screw it. I was sunk. "Well, does anybody have a brother who's knocked up his girlfriend, quit school, married her, then gone on government aid and collected food stamps instead of getting a paying job of some kind?" I waited. At first, there was silence...and then there wasn't.

"Well," Diane said, "Jenny has a brother who knocked up three girls, skipped off to Mexico and is currently serving hard time down there for bestiality. Does that count?"

"You have got to be kidding me." I understood that people had screwed-up lives, but this had to be a record in dysfunction.

"Yes!" They looked at each other and burst out laughing. While my parents wouldn't have laughed at their first little joke, I definitely wasn't laughing at this one.

Diane decided to tell me the truth, "In all seriousness, my husband is a computer programmer and my sister's an attorney. The only time I've seen her dance was at her wedding, but I'm sure she couldn't hold a candle to what I heard you did last night at the Ambassador."

"Di!" Jenny smacked her friend on the leg. "You're going to embarrass him. It's like that time you bought Jordan that bright neon thong underwear for Christmas as a gag gift."

I really didn't want to be listening to this conversation. Jordan's life was already more of an open book to me than I cared to know, and this was pushing the limits. Diane was really a bit of a sadist!

Between the little joke at my expense and the one at Jordan's, she reminded me of my bitch aunt back home. Two years ago for Christmas, Aunt Patricia gave me a four-pack of condoms in front of the entire family with "a lifetime supply for Andy" written on the box in large bold print. My response the following year was the largest pacifier I could find with "I'm sure you haven't had anything in your mouth to suck on in a long time" written on the package. Again, I was the only one laughing. I wondered how Jordan had reacted.

"He was pretty red when you did that to him," Jenny managed to get out between chuckles. "However, if I recall—and I have the pictures to prove it—you were the one who was the reddest at the end of the night when he walked out and modeled them for you in front of everybody."

"Yeah." Diane blushed. "I was. If I hadn't seen that issue of the *Advocate* on the table, I never would have known they even had rainbow thong underwear. At least the gay pride symbol is colorful, and he has such a great ass, doesn't he?" Before Jenny could reply, if she was going to at all, Diane turned around and looked at me. "Andy, if you get a chance, take a look at it. Tell us what you think."

"I am not going to look at Jordan's ass!"

"He'd probably show you before any of us again anyway," Diane teased. "And if his package is still anything like we glimpsed that night, he's going to make somebody a very happy man!"

It was obvious she knew about him after all. I wondered if there was anyone who didn't know about him. Why didn't he just take an ad out in the *New York Times* while he was at it?

"But that ass..."

"Andy's is pretty nice, too," Jenny offered, "and there are plenty of witnesses who would back that statement up."

Here was more conversation I didn't want to hear.

"Hey, maybe we should compare them to see whose is better!"

"You people have demons," I informed them matter-of-factly. So, this is what girl talk was all about? Guys discussed bust sizes and women chatted about rear ends. Was there no end to the magic of differences between the sexes? I wondered if their conversation would differ at the beach; Jordan would probably make better company for them, since all three could then discuss the asses and packages of the guys walking around. That certainly wasn't what *I* was going there for.

Jenny finally pulled onto a side street and found a parking spot. The three of us piled out, I with my towel and a book, Jenny with her towel and small bag and Diane with her towel and large bag. I was extremely curious as to what could be so important to take to the beach that required a bag the size of one I used for my laundry. I offered to carry it for her, mostly to see if I could take a peek at whatever it was, but she politely declined.

Now that we had everything, we followed Jenny as she set out towards the distant sound of waves and birds. This was going to be an extremely relaxing and monumental experience for me. I'd always wondered about the ocean and wanted to swim in it just to say I'd done it. Now that I was approaching it, though, the only thing I could think of was the movie *Jaws*. When I finally saw the water, I almost started to panic. Somewhere out there was a shark with my name on it. Maybe I'd just go in up to my knees. No, that was no good. I'd seen smaller sharks at aquariums that could survive and hunt in water that shallow. Maybe I'd just put my feet in. Wait a moment. Weren't there jellyfish in the ocean, and couldn't they sting someone into unconsciousness? Even if they couldn't, what if I was allergic to them? I would stop breathing, collapse and then the tide would carry me out to a shark.

The ocean was really losing its appeal.

I stopped a few minutes to smell the air and take a look around me. There were women everywhere! Some of them had children, so I ignored them. Some of them had boyfriends attached to their faces and waists, so I ignored them, too. Some, however, were alone and so absolutely ripe, so absolutely bursting in the bust area that I could barely contain myself. Those, I concentrated on.

Disturbingly, I didn't have the feelings of sexuality I suspected I should upon seeing breasts; mostly, I just wanted to see them jiggle and wiggle, like those Jell-O commercials. Maybe this was my second adolescence, or maybe this was just what it meant to be straight.

By the time I caught up to Jenny and Diane, they had already turned a small area of sand into a little oasis complete with a large umbrella, extra-large blankets and a tiny bar situated on a cooler. At least I now knew what she stored in that bag of hers.

Diane was making herself a daiquiri while Jenny was busy putting suntan lotion on.

"You should really put some of this on." She handed me the bottle. "Michigan must not get very much sun, considering how white you are. You'll be red as a lobster if you're not careful."

"Thanks." I started putting some on the exposed areas of my body while continuing to look around. "There are a lot of babes on this beach. This is great!"

"Yeah, I've never seen so much silicone and cases of liposuction in one place in my entire life," Diane remarked. "I hope Jenny warned you about the women around here."

"What about them?" Did they like sex to the point where they almost killed mortal men? Were they carefree to the point of just making a public spectacle of themselves while engaging in killing their men with sex? Did they have extreme grading criteria? Well, so what. None of the ripe single women on the beach today would need to employ fruit to satisfy themselves. I was here!

"They can be a little rough," Jenny cautioned me.

"Unmerciful," Diane added, "especially in today's market."

"True," Jenny agreed. "Maybe you should just stay here for a while and watch what goes on before trying anything. Have a drink with us and read a little of your book and just relax."

No way! There was no way in hell I was going to sit down and relax now that I was finally here. At least, I wasn't going to relax while I was still without the company of some fine women out for a piece of this ass people seemed to think was so nice. I didn't travel for four and a half hours by plane with a drunk grandmother who couldn't remember my name, deal with her overbearing brother and get kissed by some gay guy just to sit and read a damn book! I wanted some...some...some of what 2 Live Crew sang about in that first notorious song of theirs. This was war, and it was time for nookie!

"I think I'll just go ahead and wander around a bit and take a look at the selection. My friends back home tell me that I have a kind of charm that just attracts the beast in women." I was lying, but it sounded like the thing to say. It was an ego boost if nothing else. Now all I had to do was fool my own ego.

"Suit yourself." Diane sighed. "We'll be here when you come crying—" Jenny smacked her leg. "...crawling—" Another smack. "...walking back."

I gave them both a curious look then set out on my first expedition to score with a California woman. There were boobs as far as the eye could see, most of them pointing up towards the sky in hopes of being climbed and championed by some adventurous soul looking to share some of his spirit. Hey! That actually didn't sound so bad. Maybe I had a future in writing erotic stories. Most of those authors were writing about things they'd never experienced, and there was quite a bit I'd never experienced. As long as I could fake it like they did, there was money to be made.

The possibility of making a career out of writing about things I had no real knowledge of gave me the extra edge my self-esteem needed to include a few brunettes along with the blondes I was focusing on. There was no reason to set my sights so standard. No limits. I would just go with the flow. I'd...Whoa!

There before me under the golden sun sat someone who would be my first attempt of the day at sexual satisfaction. She was incredible! She was blond but not bleached, thin but not frail, tanned but not burned, waxed but not scarred, shaved but not cut up and, best of all, she was alone!

She was also struggling to get some suntan lotion on a part of her back that was difficult to reach. While my heart went out to her, my anatomy was strangely silent. Wake up!

"Excuse me," I greeted her, and she looked up at me. "Hi. You look like you're having some trouble, and I was wondering if I could help you with that."

"Sure," she agreed, "for ten bucks."

"Ten bucks?" My face felt like it had dropped off my head. Either she thought I was out to have sex with her or something else was going on that I wasn't aware of. Well, actually I *was* trying to have sex with her, but I think she misunderstood my intentions, if that was possible. "Wait, I'm not...Well, I mean...Why would you charge me for putting suntan lotion on you? I was only being friendly."

"You're..." Something dawned on her. "...not from around here are you?"

"No."

"I didn't think so." At least she didn't look disappointed. That gave me hope.

"Most people recognize the economy package I just offered. Either that, or they're so rich they don't even think twice about money." She looked directly at me. "Which one are you?"

"What was the middle part again?" Why should money matter? If she found me appealing and wanted to use my body for a sex toy, then more power to her. I was willing.

"Okay, I can see where this is going." She looked disappointed this time, and also appeared to be mentally storing my answers on some invisible application. This was so businesslike it was starting to scare me. "What state are you from?"

"Michigan."

"Well..." She sighed in relief, as if having solved some puzzle. "...that explains it. Aren't you guys, like, the cheese capitol of the United States?"

"That's Wisconsin," I informed her. "We've got

the Great Lakes."

"Water. It's cheaper than cheese and doesn't come in as many flavors."

It had to be easier to get a bank loan than survive an interview with this woman just to put my hand on her back and spread suntan lotion!

"What city do you live in?"

"Detroit."

"You make automobiles. Am I supposed to be impressed?" She rolled her eyes. Was it really a question?

"Yes, but we also shoot people in automobiles."

"Now I'm supposed to be impressed with violence?" She eyed me carefully.

"We also have Snooky." It was the only thing I could think of that sounded remotely impressive.

"She's just an urban legend." The girl looked a little uneasy saying that out loud—you know, just in case it wasn't true. "What's your annual income?"

"Off the scale."

"That rich?" She raised her eyebrow.

"No." I shook my head. "That poor." Next.

"Occupation?"

"Student." How could she hold getting an education against anyone? Surely this would impress her.

"Michigan State or U of M?" She had favorites.

"Grand Valley."

"How grand can it be? I've never heard of it."

Okay, enough was enough. It was obvious I'd picked a business major out looking to marry someone who would shower her with expensive gifts and take her to places I never knew existed because I couldn't afford them. Whatever happened to a man and woman meeting, liking the look of each other and then having hot, meaningless sex? The people I went to school with did it all the time. What made her so special? Did she actually have a conscience or something? And what about pity? It's not like I did this very often, or had the opportunity to.

"Let me get this straight." I looked her right in the eyes. "You're asking all these questions and using my answers as the basis of whether or not I can put suntan lotion on you?"

"No, not anymore." She peered piteously at me. "I withdraw the offer."

"You mean I don't have to pay?" This was good news. Actually, this was great news!

"No." There went the roll of the eyes. Some part of me, the realistic part, had been waiting for that to happen. "It means you no longer get to put suntan lotion on my body, period. I don't give discounts or freebies to geeky students who go to universities I've never heard of." If that wasn't cruel enough, she added, "You probably work for Kay-Mart, too." I swore right then and there that if I ever wrote a book, I'd create a character based on her and have a very cruel fate waiting just around the corner for her. "Just because I'm not as popular as some of the other girls on the beach doesn't mean I don't have a reputation to maintain."

"You mean some of the other women are more difficult than this?" I didn't even want to know.

"I didn't charge you for talking to me, did I?"

She had a point. I turned and walked away, my head hanging low. If I ever did write that book, she would have a very cruel fate, indeed. Maybe I'd have her attacked by real crabs instead of just getting a case of them. Maybe I'd have her stung by jellyfish and dragged out into the ocean and eaten by a shark. Better yet, maybe I'd have her abducted on the way back to her car by a group of motorcycle mamas who would keep her as their leather love toy. Hey, I'm for feminism!

Both Jenny and Diane read the bitterness and disappointment in my eyes well enough to know what had happened. Heck, I'm sure they knew all along what would happen, but they had the decency not to ask or rub it in.

Upon my sitting down, one put a shot of tequila in my right hand while the other sprinkled salt on my left palm. God, they were understanding! After a second shot, I decided to take their original advice and pulled out my book to read while they talked about some of the guys' packages. The words on the pages were unfortunately fuzzy, and I took a break shortly after. So much for my tolerance for alcohol.

I could still hear, though, and Jenny and Diane were having a debate about whether or not one particular guy's package was real or partially water-resistant material designed to give him that enhanced look. They both pulled out binoculars, and I was forced to tune them out when they started talking about what natural wrinkles on a man's...

Well, what they looked like versus the suspected fake material.

It was my impression that the debate ended a short time later when another unknowing subject walked by and they concentrated on him.

Apparently, there were so many of these men they couldn't remember what they'd decided about the first guy when I inquired later on as we were leaving.

I may not have met any more women, but I did finally get some reading done as soon as my vision cleared. Feeding my brain was probably the smart thing to do, since crushing my ego any further might have actually led to a depression. I didn't come all this way to be depressed. Tomorrow was a new day, and maybe I'd score then.

❧ ❧ ❧

We dropped Diane off then picked up Kenny. Jordan was cooking some burgers for himself and the kids when we ran in to quickly change clothes. He didn't say a word to me nor did he make direct eye contact. I really must have hit a nerve with him earlier, but there wasn't a chance to take him aside and tell him I was sorry before we were running back out the door again to hit Tower Records and then stop somewhere for dinner.

It didn't feel right to me to leave bad feelings between us. Just because he was gay didn't mean he didn't have feelings. That thought struck me almost as a revelation. I guess I never thought of it that way, that someone considered so deviant could also be human, that they really did have feelings. Of course, this revelation did absolutely nothing to make me feel better. It made it worse.

I'd learned two ways to beat a guilt trip in all my years of screwing things up. The first was to apologize to the person and try to right the wrong. The second was to go out and buy music! Considering the number of CDs and tapes I owned, I was going to hell.

155

Since I wasn't able to talk to Jordan this evening, I would have to do it tomorrow; but I still felt bad. This setback only allowed me to justify buying music tonight so I would feel better.

Tower Records was everything they'd promised me it would be. What I really liked about it, besides the selection, was that it was cheaper than Harmony House. Of course, these days, what wasn't? I picked up some Bronski Beat, Pet Shop Boys and Erasure while Jenny and Kenny bought some Paul McCartney, Rolling Stones and Don Henley. Their selections didn't thrill me as much as the ones I picked up, but I liked Don Henley well enough. I think my tastes had changed a bit since the Go-Gos had broken up.

New groups were appealing to me, and I couldn't put my finger on why. Maybe it was the synth sound, the oddly compelling lyrics or something in the singers' voices. I really didn't know.

We headed out, after spending more than an hour in the store, for a Mexican restaurant they told me was to die for. I promised myself I was going to remember it this time. I also promised I wasn't going to drink, which is how I intended on remembering it.

The great thing about making promises to yourself is that they're like New Year's resolutions—bound to be broken sooner or later, and who would really know? I remembered the restaurant coming home, so I'd at least upheld half the promises to myself. The rest was drowned in a Corona with a half-piece of lime still stuck in the neck of the bottle. Unbeknownst to me, the other half of the lime was still stuck between my teeth.

Drinking is so not worth it.

7

The black-and-white waiting area was a bustle of activity. Students with gray backpacks flowed from one side of the room to the other. Some disappeared around a corner then reappeared moments later outside the large panoramic window I sat in front of while others walked inside offices, doors closing behind them. When the doors reopened, the students were gone as if they had never been there at all. I felt oddly like a character in a David Lynch film. What had they been doing, and where had they gone?

The woman sitting at the reception desk didn't seem to take any notice at all, so maybe this was a normal occurrence.

I glanced over at a table next to me. On top of a number of magazines like *Sports Illustrated*, *Time* and *Consumer Reports* was a class catalogue for UCLA.

That's right! Diane had suggested I consider transferring out to California to the university where Jordan went. *That's* what I was doing, checking to see what program would be best for me.

It was funny how I couldn't remember something as simple as that. I definitely needed to stay focused if I was going to look into their English department and find out what it had to offer me.

"Andy Stevenson?" the receptionist called. "Reverend Shelton will see you now."

"Thank you." I stood up and crossed to the office she was pointing to. Reverend? Why would there be a reverend in charge of recruiting students? Still, but it couldn't hurt to talk to him. He was obviously in that position for a reason.

I entered to find myself in a very large chapel, hardly what I was expecting. I turned around to see how all of this fit into a building that seemed quite a bit smaller from the outside, but the entrance was no longer there. Whatever. I was a writer, not an architect.

At the very front of the chapel, just in front of the altar, was a long desk with a man seated behind it flipping through some papers. Some of them must have been important because he spoke up and blessed one every once in a while.

"Please, my son..." Reverend Shelton looked up at me. "...come in and sit down. May I offer you some holy water or a communion wafer?"

"Thank you, no. I try not to snack between meals." I walked to the desk and sat in a chair I hadn't noticed before. "I didn't think ministers gave out communion wafers."

"Generally, we don't. However, we're quite well-stocked, and it beats offering guilt trips and Hail Marys."

"Good point." I had to give him credit for thinking of that one. What did he offer Buddhists?

It must have been something they didn't have to worry about coming back as in their next life.

"Now, what troubles you?" He got right to the point.

"Nothing is bothering me. I was just entertaining thoughts about transferring out here from back home. I had questions and wanted to check into what kinds of programs were available."

Maybe the appointment person had made an error and sent me to the wrong counselor.

"Oh!" Reverend Shelton perked up. "That's right. You must be Andy." He shuffled through some more papers until he found the one he wanted. "The appointment person made a mistake in sending you to me." Well, that made sense. "I generally deal with the majority of the student body," he explained. "Those who are wholesome, pure, virtuous and straight."

"It's amazing you have any appointments at all." I laughed softly. The reverend didn't seem too amused. "Uh, anyway, I'm fairly wholesome, pure—in body, at least—and very straight about what program I want to graduate in."

"I'm sorry," he interrupted, "but you're going to have to talk to one of our special counselors, one who is trained in dealing with your kind."

"My kind? You mean transfer students?"

He gave me a look as if to say I knew *exactly* what he was talking about and it wasn't that.

"I'm a little lost here."

"I know you're lost, my son." Reverend Shelton looked said and pointed to a door that had appeared to my left. "Go through there, and may God be with you and show you back to His kingdom."

"Thanks." What a strange way for him to end our conversation.

I hadn't realized I was so far off the path in life God wanted me to follow. The reverend apparently had a paper that said so, though, so it must be true. Isn't that the way it worked with religion? It was printed somewhere and therefore must be true?

I stood up and started towards the door. Just before I opened it, I turned back around and could swear I saw the reverend shaking his head at my paper and mumbling something that sounded vaguely like "unholy." Since when did the Church dislike English majors?

The next room turned out to be another waiting room, though it was very different from the first one I'd been in. For one, it wasn't all black and white. Colorful rainbows decorated these walls, and there were triangular chairs spread throughout the room. Even the pencils and pens lying on the receptionist's desk were the same colors found in the rest of the room. Was this the daycare part of the building? If the appointment person had made another mistake, they were going to hear about it!

"Andy?" A man poked his head out from one of two office doors, and I nodded. "Why don't you have a seat. I'm just finishing up with your sponsor, and then we'll get you in here in a moment."

"Okay." Sponsor? What sponsor? I didn't realize I needed one and certainly never knew I had one. This whole procedure was entirely ridiculous. All I wanted to do was find out if the damn university had anything to offer me or not. The way things stood, I was more than content to go back to the cornfields, the smell of fertilizer and anti-

McDonalds campaigns.

I sat down impatiently and looked around for a magazine, hoping *Time* had a movie review I hadn't read.

"Holy..."

The magazines were as different in this waiting room as the waiting room itself. Instead of the respectable and recognizable titles I'd seen earlier, there were copies of *Advocate* and, most unexpectedly, *Playgirl*. I wondered if the receptionist or counselor knew they were out here. Someone was obviously playing a prank, so maybe I should get rid of them, or at least bring it to their attention. If this area did house a daycare program, I was certain parents wouldn't want their children looking at a magazine like that.

"I think we have things well in hand." The man who had spoken before appeared next to me. "You can come on in now."

"Great." That hadn't taken as long as I thought it would. I stood up and followed him back into his office. "Listen, just so you know, uh, somebody stuck a *Playgirl* magazine out there on the table."

"I know." He looked at me slyly. "It's the Mel Gibson issue. I'm surprised no one's stolen it yet. Have a seat."

I sat down in one of the triangular rainbow-colored chairs as he took his place on the other side of the desk. Whoever my sponsor was, he or she was no longer in the room. That was really the least of my worries. What bothered me was that the counselor knew exactly what issue the *Playgirl* was and expressed surprise not at the fact it was out there in the open, but that no one had stolen it. I understood that UCLA was liberal, but I had no idea just how liberal. Furthermore, I knew Mel Gibson enjoyed showing off his bottom in movies, but I'd never heard of him showing it off in glossy print.

"Look," I began, "I'll make this simple. I don't want holy water, communion wafers or a look at Mel Gibson's ass or any other private areas. All I want to know is how good your English program is in case, however unlikely, I should decide to transfer."

"Oh," the counselor scoffed, "we've already dispensed with that major and chosen the appropriate one for you. Now, if you'll just take a look at these—"

"Excuse me?" I cut him off. "You and somebody else dispensed with my major? This decision was made for me and without my consent?"

I had no idea what to say to this. These people had some nerve.

The counselor was peering at me, uncertain why I was balking.

"Did it occur to anyone that I might actually like English and be fairly proficient at it?"

"Well," the man piped up, "of course we took that into consideration. Consider this, however. Why limit yourself to just English?" He was starting to become enthusiastic. "Why not embrace the shoes of the major you were born to fill instead? Why not follow the road you have always naturally and instinctively known you should be traveling?"

"Don't even say chemistry," I warned.

"No, not that." He chuckled. "Not chemistry."

"Then what? What?" I demanded. "What major

am I so well suited for? Huh?"

"Homosexuality!" he exclaimed triumphantly.

"That's not a major." I sat back in the chair in disgust. "It's a lifestyle, and a lifestyle by choice. That means I have a choice in this matter, and I choose not to bother with it. I mean..." I snorted in exasperation. "...what kind of courses could possibly be offered for such a ridiculous curriculum?"

Oh, I could see it now. The first one would start off with basic stuff, like color identification. No longer could I say something was yellow, dark green, beige, blue, orange or light green. It would be lemon, kiwi, taupe, turquoise, crush and lime from here on out. I don't think so!

"That's the beauty of the major, though." The counselor pulled a catalogue out of his desk and opened it to some page I couldn't see. "There aren't any what you might call regular courses offered."

"Then what kind are there?"

"Intercourses!"

He had to be kidding.

"There're two major areas you have to pass in the intercourses, only it doesn't matter which you take first. One is the Oral Intercourse, which consists of the Amateur, Competent and VHS-Friendly levels. We have several electives available for the Oral area, including..." He searched a few pages further in the book. "...the Gag Reflex, Tongue—Instrument of Pleasure, and Ingestion."

"Oh, those are so important in life," I muttered as sarcastically as I possibly could.

"You know it!" He completely ignored my attitude and pressed on. "The second intercourse is a real favorite of students: Anal. Unfortunately, not everybody is cut out for the Anal Intercourse, and most of the ones who aren't don't make it past Penetration, the first level. Once you get to Depth Perception, the second level, those who are there are in it for keeps. The third level, obviously, is Diddling."

"Obviously."

"And the electives..."

"I can hardly wait."

"...are High-Octane Lubrication, Frequent Frantic Fornicating and The Bald—"

"I get the point," I interrupted, "or at least a picture that comes to mind. I don't think I need to know more."

"So." He pulled some papers out of his desk and laid them down in front of me. "The sooner we get you processed and enrolled, the sooner you can start your new life and I can pick up my free microwave oven." The counselor seemed overjoyed at the prospect of claiming his prize. "Now, if I can get five more people, I'll be eligible for a trip for two to Hawaii!"

"Hawaii? There aren't any—wait a second." I objected. "I'm not signing anything, so you can hold off on that microwave."

"Andy." He seemed saddened by my attitude. "We don't need you to sign on the dotted line right now."

I was relieved. This might buy me enough time to escape from his office and get the hell back home where I belonged.

"You signed it before you were even born. This isn't a choice or lifestyle. It's the way things really are, who you really are. Andy Stevenson, this is your life! You just have to acknowledge it to start."

"Look, for the last time, I'm *not* gay!"

"Sure you're not, Andy." The counselor winked at me. "And neither is Nathan Lane or Elton John."

"They aren't gay." Nathan Lane? Oh, come on! Well, maybe. And Elton John was just a bit peculiar in his outfits and such. He couldn't possibly be gay. Hell, he was about as likely to be "festive" as...that one guy who starred in the movie *Hearts Of Fire* with Fiona and Bob Dylan. What was his name again? Rupert Everett!

"You're so closeted you can't see what's in front of your face."

"Excuse me?" It occurred to me suddenly that this was all just a dream. I didn't have to be here. I didn't have to stay. "I don't have to take this."

He looked at me with sad eyes again.

"In fact, I'm going to wake up now."

"Yes." He smiled gently. "I believe you will."

❦ ❦ ❦

I think Jenny sensed there was something wrong between Jordan and I. Almost anyone else would have chalked it up to a personality conflict mixed with some overt hostility, but not her. Jordan was a good kid and, as far she knew, so was I, therefore it must be something other than boys just being boys—or boys doing boys in Jordan's case although he hadn't "done" me.

There was a reason for the tension, and Jenny was bound and determined to see us work it out whether we wanted to or not. Her plan was simple. Jordan had an errand to run in the morning and was going to meet up with us at a restaurant near the beach in the afternoon, only Jenny had no intention of making it a group event. No sooner had we pulled into the parking lot when her pager went off. She excused herself to use a payphone then reappeared a few minutes later.

"Andy." She put on her best apologetic face. "That was Kenny. My dear absent-minded husband seems to have left his briefcase at home and—"

"No, he didn't," Benny interrupted.

"Yes...he...did." She stared him down then turned back to me. "And I have to go take it to him. Someone's going to have to wait for Jordan, though, so..."

"No, he *didn't*," Lenny chimed in.

"Do you both like living?" Jenny raised her voice, and they immediately nodded that they did, indeed. "Now, what did I just say?"

"Daddy left his briefcase at home," Benny repeated.

"And Andy has to wait here for Jordan," Lenny finished.

"That's right," She growled at them, then looked back at me with the sweetest of smiles. "Would you be a dear and wait here for Jordan? He doesn't have a pager, and I don't want him to think that something happened to us. Here." She pulled a twenty out of her purse and forced it into my hand. "Go grab something to eat, and we'll catch up with you later."

She shooed the kids back into the minivan, tossed my bag out the window and was backing out of the space before I even had a chance to respond.

I knew a set-up when I saw one, but they were generally a bit more subtle than this. What could I do except stand there with a dumbfounded look on my face and wonder what the hell had just happened? I threw my hands up in the air in a desperate attempt to express absolutely nothing that came to mind then headed for the entrance. At least I'd eat.

It was one of those restaurants that served a little bit of everything, didn't specialize in anything and made it all just a little bit differently so that they could call it "California cuisine." Well, that's how I interpreted it, anyway. I ended up with something that was called a "BLT" yet was anything but a BLT. Bean sprouts, lox and tangelos just wasn't the same as bacon, lettuce and tomatoes, but it was my own fault for not reading the description. Who knew?

I looked around for a place to sit and actually expected to find one. Forget for a moment that it was lunchtime, and that all the kids were out of school and it was a beautiful day outside. After all, I was certain people had better things to do than eat at this very same restaurant and take up all the tables at the very moment I was looking for one. Right, and it was just a rumor that people went out shopping the day after Thanksgiving.

"Hey, Detroit!" a voice called out. I turned towards the sound on the chance that whoever it was might actually mean me. Sure enough, sitting at a table by herself and finishing up some peach cobbler while reading a book was the girl from the beach the previous day who'd wanted to charge me ten dollars to put suntan lotion on her. She waved for to me to come over. Like an idiot, I did.

"I just used up most of my cash and I didn't bring

the checkbook," I told her sarcastically, "so I don't know if I can afford to sit here."

"That's okay," she assured me and winked. "I'm not charging."

"What?" I looked at her in mock surprise. "Tips were good yesterday?"

"I'm not a prostitute." She didn't sound amused.

"True. I'd have been the one getting screwed," I muttered just loud enough for her to hear. "May I sit down?"

"Go ahead, Detroit," she replied evenly. "I'm Janice, by the way."

"I'm Andy." I sat down and spread a napkin across my lap. "Everyone else seems to call me something else, so if you want to call me 'Detroit,' I'll answer to that, too. What are you reading?"

"*The Wolf and The Dove* by Kathleen Woodewiss." Janice watched my face twitch. "Is there a problem?"

"That book just isn't my idea of romance." I knew because I'd bought all of Woodewiss's books for my mother for her birthday and Christmas. While I hadn't actually read them, I did skim them and read the back covers. "If some guy invading a woman's world, and her wanting to kill him and then ending up finding herself attracted to him does it for you, fine. I'd hardly call that love, though."

"Sure, and you were looking for romance and love yesterday at the beach, weren't you?"

Okay, she had a point.

"Did you know that most tourists come here because they think California women are so desperate for sex that we'll employ fruit when we can't get a man?"

"I've...never heard that before." My face said differently.

"I wonder where people get these ideas from sometimes." She looked around the room and shook her head. "Like I have nothing better to do with my life than think about sex twenty-four hours a day, seven days a week. Believe me, I can't stand it when men stare at my boobs and think because I'm blond that I want to be..." She paused. "How do they put it? 'Championed by some adventurous soul looking to share some of his...'"

"Spirit?" I suggested. That sounded really familiar to me. Maybe I wasn't meant to be a romance writer after all. I mean, if she could come up with the same wording I did...

"Exactly. I mean, who talks like that, anyway?"

Did she expect me to answer that? I hoped not.

"Let me offer you some insight," she went on. "You have no idea what it's like to be undressed in the daydreams of every guy who walks by, and looked upon solely as an object of sexual desire. I want to be seen as someone much more. I have brains, dreams, wants, needs, desires of my own, and I want someone to love me for more than the sum of my outer beauty.

"Just because someone approaches me doesn't mean I'm going to like them, but you wouldn't believe the things they say if I don't think their pick-up lines are the wittiest and most charming things I've ever heard. Most of the time when I do date, they're only interested in one thing. Now, not all of them are assholes, but enough of them."

Several long moments of silence passed before

she got curious enough to wonder what I was thinking.

"Well?"

"I'm still a little stuck on me not having any idea what it's like to be undressed in someone's day-dreams and looked upon as an object of sexual desire."

She didn't know about Jordan.

"You've just completely missed the entire point of the conversation." Janice sighed, took a bite of her cobbler and picked her book back up. "Eat your lunch."

"I'm not totally missing the point." I picked my sandwich up and took a bite. "Oh, what the hell!" I grimaced. "This is disgusting!"

"You should have asked them to put avocado on it."

"This was one of the few things I didn't think would *have* avocado." I picked up a French fry and tested it to make sure it really was a French fry and not some other funky thing. It was real. "Anyway, it's not like what you were saying is the first time I've ever heard that, and it's not like I don't have insight into people, either. I'm not completely shallow."

"Well." Janice set her book back down. "By all means, please share this brilliant insight with me."

"Fine. I will." I looked around and gathered my thoughts, except there weren't any. "People are like..." My eyes finally rested on..."French fries."

"That's your insight? An analogy that people are like French fries?" She stared at me, but couldn't figure out if I was telling her the truth or pulling this out of my ass. I think it was the uncertainty that prompted her to let me continue. "Okay, how?"

Yeah, genius, how?

This was going well. Janice had actually thought enough to ask me to sit down so she could share some of her insight with me, and I was paying her back with ca-ca. It was my duty as a writer to be thorough in all forms of thought and quick tidbits of wisdom, including such subjects as love, romance and the binding energy that brought the people of the world together.

It was also my duty to be able to bullshit when necessary.

"I think it's the potato that's important as opposed to strictly the fry itself."

Janice gave me a perplexed look.

"They're like parts...parts that make up the whole. For instance, we eat French fries with salt and ketchup, but you wouldn't do that with a baked potato. Most people eat that with butter and sometimes sour cream, but not ketchup. Likewise, we don't smother French fries with butter or sour cream. Do you follow me?"

She didn't.

"Okay, take home fries or hash browns, now. We have ketchup with those, but no sour cream. Sometimes we even butter them or add eggs, but you wouldn't add eggs to a baked potato. We also wouldn't have eggs with French fries, but we would the hash browns. Then you get into combinations like potato salad, which has salad dressing as opposed to sour cream. I mean, they're both white substances, but miles apart in taste and compatibility. When was the last time you had salad dressing with a baked potato or a French fry?

171

It would be like mayonnaise instead of vanilla sauce on your cobbler."

"What the hell are you talking about?" Janice kept looking at her cobbler, my fries and then finally back at me. "You didn't just think of that, did you? I mean, you couldn't have." She sounded frustrated. "I mean, what the hell are you talking about?"

"People, Janice. Remember?" I stared into her eyes. "Think of the potatoes as people. They come in all shapes, sizes, colors, et cetera, but deep down they're still potatoes."

"People."

"People, yes. You're getting it." Well, I'm glad *she* was because I was starting to feel a little lost. If only I could pull this one off. "You see? It doesn't matter what we look like, what we sound like or how popular we are because we're all people." I think I was finally driving my point home. "As people, we need to get past the colors of our skin. We need to get past this whole fashion thing and see people for who they are inside. We need to be more helpful than hateful. We need—"

"Oh, my God!" Janice interrupted. "You're *gay*."

"Excuse me?" Exactly how had she come to that conclusion?

"You *are*." She paused. "I should have figured it out yesterday at the beach, only you couldn't take your eyes off my breasts. I keep forgetting that just because you guys don't want to have sex with women doesn't mean you don't appreciate the female form."

"*What?*"

"Come on, Detroit. Straight guys don't talk like

172

you do." Janice rolled her eyes. "We need to be more helpful than hateful? You don't strike me as a politician, and you're a little too open about being respectful and unprejudiced towards people of ethnicity, not to mention your desire to see past materialism. Did you just come out of the closet?"

"Come out of the closet? Is that the same thing as coming out from under a rock?" When was it, exactly, that I had lost control of the conversation here? I realized I had gone about my point in a roundabout way, but for her to get this interpretation was beyond ridiculous. "I don't understand this. You assumed I was coming on to you yesterday and gave me an earful about it. When we have a real conversation today and I *don't* come on to you, you now assume that I must be gay. For someone so big on insight, you're basing a whole lot of yours on assumption."

"Fair enough," Janice conceded. "Let's just do this the direct way, then. Are you gay?"

"No." That was easy enough. See? I answered the question without hesitation, so she shouldn't have any reason to doubt me.

"Have you ever had sex with a man?"

"That is *so* none of your business." Okay, that caught me off-guard, and I felt my face become rather hot rather quickly.

"That's a yes." Janice sat back in her chair. "Okay, so you're not gay, but you've had sex with men. I take it, then, that you've had sex with women, too?" She stared at me expectantly.

"That's also none of your business." Okay, reverse psychology. If the first time I said it meant yes, then it should work the same way the second time.

"That's a no, which would indicate that you aren't exactly bi." Now she leaned forward again. "I'm confused, Detroit. You say you're not gay, yet you've only had sex with men. Do you not see a pattern here? Now, if I'm assuming too much, then maybe *you* should do the math."

"Okay, fine." I sighed. "You caught me. I'll admit it, but only to you." I leaned in close enough to her so she wouldn't have any trouble hearing me at all. "*I'm straight!*" She jumped. "Is that clear enough for you?"

"Hey, sexy." A voice behind me spoke up. "Where are Aunt Jenny and the kids?"

My lip involuntarily curled. Yep, Jordan had arrived and was speaking to me again.

"Don't say it," I warned Janice before she could even open her mouth. "Not one word." With that, I stood up, grabbed my tray and headed for the garbage.

"Aren't you going to finish your sandwich?" Jordan asked as he followed me.

"Nope. It tastes like crap anyway." I dumped it into the trash.

"You should have asked them to put avocado on it." Was he being helpful or trying to pull my strings? "And where's Aunt Jenny? You never answered me. What was up with that girl back there? Were you trying to score or something? Because it didn't look like she was buying it." Yep, he was trying to pull my strings. "What pickup line did you use? I might be able to tell you if it would have worked on me. And—"

"Shut up!"

❧ ❧ ❧

174

The beach was fairly crowded again and there were a number of women walking around, but that was about all I noticed. It wasn't anything like the previous day where I was attempting to judge if their breasts had silicone in them or listening to Jenny and Diane determine if the men were taking steroids and stuffing their thongs with enough water-resistant material to make them look like they had more of a package than they actually did. I just didn't care today.

Jordan and I strolled down by the water and steered towards one of the farthest areas, where there weren't as many people. I didn't know if he could explain the two dreams I'd had since arriving in California, but I couldn't just ignore them or the potential to figure out what they meant. Something was going on, and I didn't know what it was. I also needed to apologize to him.

He broke the silence. "You're kind of quiet. I thought maybe something was on your—"

"Are there gays in Hawaii?" That question had been on my mind since the counselor in my dream had mentioned a vacation for two there. Hawaii was such a small place I couldn't imagine there could possibly be any gay people there. Wasn't the statistic, like, one in every ten million or something? Since I knew of my two cousins from the anniversary party and then Jordan, that pretty much took care of this part of California.

"Andy, there are gays everywhere."

My question seemed to amuse him to no end. I didn't want to admit it, certainly not to him, but I was glad. Maybe he'd forgive me for what I'd said to him the previous day.

"Are there classes about being gay?" There couldn't be, could there? Not really. "I mean, I feel stupid for asking this, but I was just wondering. Heterosexual sex is kind of taught in health classes, but I've never seen anything about gay sex." I didn't know what else to call it. Heck, I didn't even think I knew the language. "I just wondered if they teach it at the college level or if it's something you have to pick up by yourself."

"Are you interested in learning about—"

"Don't even start with that line of thinking!" I should have known he wouldn't have been able to resist making a comment like that. "I'm confident enough in my own sexuality that I felt I could ask you that without you taking it the wrong way."

I wasn't, of course, but that was beside the point. I was more concerned with what *he* was more hung up about. Me? Or sex?

"And you know what? It's comments like that make me believe gay society and culture is based almost entirely on sex. Is it really like that?"

"You sound like my parents." Jordan winced. It must have been a bad memory for him. I thought he might lash out at me again for saying something potentially offensive, but he looked thoughtful instead. "What do you know about gay culture?"

"Not much, really." It was only fair to admit the limits of my knowledge. Besides, I was tired of looking stupid when I was with him. "I know it started with the Greeks." Weren't they some warrior race who weren't allowed to have sex with women unless the match was approved by some council? Even then the actual mating was witnessed, which would be enough to make even the most chaste of men look for an alternative. Who would have thought one could get some kind of satisfaction from one's fellow warriors in the bath? Hey! I wondered if that was where the term *bathhouse* originated.

"And that gay people started fighting for equal rights after Stonehenge."

"Stonewall."

"Whatever."

"And, by the way, I think you mean the Romans."

"There's a diff..." Was there really a difference, and did I really want to look stupid again? "That's what I meant." I sat down on the sand and watched the waves come lapping up at my feet. It struck me that this should be a moment I'd make an effort to remember, because I'd never felt the ocean on my skin before. I'd been to lakes and swimming pools, but never had I been in touch with a part of something so vast I could barely imagine. I'd been alive longer than most swimming pools, but not the ocean, and who knew what secrets it could tell?

Jordan sat down next to me and looked into the distance, perhaps sensing the same things I was. Here was history, and the future. Actually, the history part reminded me of something.

"I think I once read somewhere that someone, Richard the Great, maybe, might have been gay."

"There is no Richard the Great." He gave me a bewildered glance. "You're thinking of Alexander...and why do you think his men called him 'Great?'"

I looked over at him and he at me, then we both started laughing out loud. It was a healthy feeling and release, so I didn't mind it so much. God, I'm so anal-retentive! Why did I have to keep pushing, and consider whether every little gesture, phrase or response could be misinterpreted as an invitation to invade my personal space?

Jordan and I knew exactly where we stood with each other, and he was just having a little bit of fun with me with some of his more suggestive comments, something no different than what I'd done with friends in that past. Hell, his response about Richard the Great would have been one I would have given. Maybe I was still too scared to admit similarities we really did have.

"So." I had so many questions I still wanted to ask him. "Why did your parents kick you out?" It was a bit personal, but I didn't think he'd mind.

"Because I'm gay."

I could have guessed as much, but I knew there had to be more to it than that.

"They just couldn't stand their only son being as interested in men as their daughter was." The definite sound of mischief was in his voice. "Bringing our dates home for dinner on the same night caused a bit of tension." He suddenly sobered. "Which turned out to be the last straw."

"I've had a few last straws myself—a lot of them, actually, but not in the same way as you." His was definitely a lot more serious than my sticking a nail through a glove and putting ketchup around it. "It could have been worse if you and your sister were supposed to double date and then discovered when he arrived that you were seeing the same person."

We both chuckled.

"Of course, your taste in men is questionable at

best, anyway."

"What do you mean by that?" Jordan took his T-shirt off, put it behind his head, lay down and closed his eyes. He had a nice chest, with just enough muscle one could trace what I recalled Jenny terming a "six-pack." There wasn't much hair on it, which was probably a plus for him since it meant no hair on his back. Women on radio call-in shows always complained about guys with hairy backs and arms and what a turnoff it was. I just thanked God I didn't have that problem.

Hell, I never had my shirt off for women to see my chest or back, anyway. They had it difficult, too, however, and I was glad I didn't have to shave my legs or under my arms.

It was still irritating to me that Jordan was as attractive as he was, especially with his unblemished and tanned skin. *Do you have any idea how much I wish my body looked like yours? Do you know how satisfied I could be to go out with someone with a body like yours? Having everyone around me envious and knowing that I was the only one who would get to go home and rest my chin on your chest or fall asleep wrapped up in your arms...*

I suddenly felt rather uncomfortable. Oh, shit! Pain! Claustrophobic swimming trunks! Ouch! Look away from Jordan! Claustrophobic swimming trunks! Just pull your T-shirt down...There you go. That's better. Act natural. Act normal. No one saw or suspected, not even Jordan. Remember to breathe. That's it. Nice and regular...Relax...

My imagination really needs a tether. Next thing I know, I'll be talking to myself...Just think about nuns for a moment or Grandma. That should do the

179

trick. Just imagine Grandma talking to Roberto about...oral sex. That's definitely a disgusting thought. Heck, oral sex was disgusting enough in itself, let alone Grandma talking about it. What was oral sex, anyway? Foreplay? Well, if foreplay was a precursor to sex, then what led up to foreplay? What part of the human body stimulated such an act?

I looked over at Jordan again. Well, he has a small patch of hair reaching its way up from below his navel that thins out just a little ways above it. There's a term for that I've heard. What was it again? Women like to start off at the top of it and work their way down. Oh, I remember now!

"What?" Jordan opened his eyes and looked at me.

"Highway to heaven!" I announced triumphantly.

"Huh?" He looked confused. "What's highway to heaven?"

"Oh, it's the patch of..." It suddenly dawned on me that I'd said it out loud. Dumb! Dumb! Dumb! Stupid! "Nothing." My voice cracked, and I forced a smile on my face that I hoped didn't look too stupid or fake. "I was just thinking..." Why bother explaining? "Nothing. Never mind." Well, I'd better say something now. "I was just feeling...I was just looking...out at the ocean, and this one patch of sky out there reminded me of the opening credit sequence on that show with Michael Landon."

"Oh." He shrugged. "I thought you were talking about the patch of hair I have from my groin to just above my navel."

I think my eyes grew large and round, but I can't be sure. It felt like I'd been caught doing something

I had no business doing, only I doubted Jordan would have minded this particular trespass.

"What did you mean when you said I had questionable taste in men? You never answered me the first time I asked." He closed his eyes again.

"Right." Did this constitute putting my foot in my mouth or my entire leg? "I guess I meant that it seems to me you don't have the best luck picking out men. Hell, you came on to me the other night at the party."

Creases appeared in his forehead.

"I just chalked it up to you being either desperate or drunk." I laughed nervously.

"You have a self-esteem problem," he informed me.

"No, I'm just in touch with reality." I fought off a growing need for distance between us again. "I'm aware of my limitations, and it doesn't hurt my feelings to acknowledge that it's a rare occurrence when someone is sanely or soberly interested in me. End of discussion on that topic."

The last thing I wanted him doing was dissecting that part of my life. It didn't mean, however, that I couldn't dissect his.

"Have you dated a lot of guys?"

"Dated? Yes." He chuckled. "It's not exactly an uncommon occurrence out here, so..."

"So?" I pressed.

"So, this conversation would probably start leaning in the direction of gay culture again and you're not exactly comfortable with that subject." Jordan folded his hands on his chest. "It's all about sex, remember?"

"You're telling me that sex has nothing to do

with it?" Did he think I was some kind of an idiot? Then too, based on some of the really stupid things I'd said to him in the past three days, I wouldn't be the least bit surprised if he *did* think I was a total idiot—or at least a bit on the moronic side.

"Sure it does, and I'd be lying if I said it didn't, but it isn't *just* sex." He sat up on his elbows now and addressed me. "It's also about self-identity, identity within the larger society, the right to have a philosophy that differs from the majority and the right to tolerance of that philosophy and self from the majority—the right to be who one really is."

"And the right for men to dress up in women's clothes and act like women? The right to lust after children? The right to pursue and use any means necessary to seduce those who may not feel the same way?"

It was harsh, but it was an argument I'd never heard played out from a gay viewpoint before. Besides, I wanted to know. Some part of me *needed* to know.

"Haven't you heard anything I've just been telling you?" Jordan's face was red with anger. "Do you have any idea how often people have thrown those same accusations at me? My parents said the same things."

I didn't know if he was going to finish or not. Finally, he continued.

"If men want to dress up like women, so what? Is it harming you in any way? Are they calling you on the phone or showing up on your porch asking you to join in? I've never done that. Does that mean I'm no longer allowed to be gay? I don't think so, Andy." He was really getting red in the face. Maybe I should have brought these things up to him a different way. "And try this one. Did you know that the majority of child molesters are *hetero*sexual? It's a statistical fact. I've certainly never tried to take advantage of a minor in my twenty-two years of life, even when I was a minor, but I've heard about it being done. Do I agree with it? Absolutely not! That's not the kind of person I am.

"And as for seducing people, there's as much seduction going on in the straight bars as there is in any gay bar I've ever been to. Men can be assholes no matter what their sexual orientation is, so sometimes the word *no* doesn't work in any bar or situation in life. And...And..."

And? And what? Why had he stopped?

Jordan's attention was suddenly somewhere else, somewhere toward the main area of the beach behind me. I turned and saw three young women in bikinis walking toward us, one of them occasionally pointing our way and saying something to the others. What the hell was this all about?

It seemed Jordan didn't know, either, which is why he apparently thought it best to save whatever else it was he intended to say until later. I thought at first maybe it was a friend of his, either from school or from his summer job, but I changed my mind. I sure as heck didn't recognize them, though I can say I wouldn't have minded if I had.

They finally got close enough to have a normal conversation without shouting.

"Hi!" the one in the middle, petite and extremely attractive, greeted me. I was at a total loss why she would be talking to me let alone being pleasant. "You probably don't remember me from the other night."

"Are you sure you have the right person?" I figured she had to be confusing me with somebody else. If I'd been with her "the other night," I'm sure I would have remembered it.

"Oh, yeah." she replied enthusiastically. "I–I didn't mean to interrupt you and your friend or anything."

Why did she seem so nervous, like I was a movie actor or someone important like that?

"My name's Angela, and I just wanted to say that I loved your show! I've been telling all my friends about it." She motioned to the two girls on either side of her. Both were equally good-looking and worthy of any male's attention.

"My show?" Now I was really confused.

"The other night at the Ambassador, when you sang 'Touch Me' and 'Boom Boom.'"

"Oh, that show." This could only happen to me. Of all the beaches in the LA area, I had to run into someone who saw me give a performance I couldn't remember at a bar I couldn't recall on a night I had no recollection of. Just as long as she didn't bring up the other part of my show…"Well, thank you." I hoped she would go away now. While I enjoyed the attention of beautiful women, I didn't enjoy *this* kind of attention. "I can't imagine my singing was very good, but then, I was a bit intoxicated."

"The singing wasn't as bad as you think." Angela sounded quite impressed. "You had a lot of energy on the stage, and the crowd really felt it. I know I did."

Okay, she'd made her point and could leave any time now.

"Especially when you showed that ass of yours! It was like 'Oh. My, God!' I just wanted to reach up and grab it!" The other two girls giggled. "I don't want to embarrass you..."

"Perish the thought." Gee, it was already a bit late for that.

How in the hell was I ever going to grow as a person with reminders of just how immature I could be popping up and hindering me? I wondered what Jordan thought about all of this. He was staying rather quiet, but I couldn't find an excuse to turn around and gauge his expression and see if he was amused, indifferent or embarrassed, like I was. Why he would be embarrassed I had no idea, but he could at least fake it for my sake.

"I just wanted to tell you how much I liked what you did up there and how gorgeous an ass you have."

Before I had a chance to respond to her statement, another voice joined the conversation.

"I hear his ass is nothing compared to his front," Jordan chimed in. God help him when the girls were gone because I was going to kill him!

"I'll bet. Well...bye." Angela looked me over once more before turning around and starting back the way they had come. I was still too shocked at what Jordan had said to return the farewell.

One of Angela's friends would sneak a glance back at me every once in a while. What they were expecting to see, and why people in this state constantly looked everyone else over I'll never know. I just hoped they didn't think I was going to give them a free peepshow because I was too damn busy planning a homicide!

"Nothing compared to my *front?*" I turned and glared at him. "Thanks for your input. I'm sure I couldn't have handled those women without you."

I shook my head, still finding it hard to believe he'd said that.

Jordan was once again very amused at my expense.

"Just where did you get an idea like that, anyway? No, wait! I don't want to know."

He stood up and walked a little ways out into the water, still grinning from ear to ear.

"And you can quit grinning!"

That only made him laugh.

"How would you like it if I dragged you out into the water and dunked it off?"

"Anytime you're feeling froggy..." He could hardly stop laughing long enough to talk. "...just jump." He obviously didn't fear any reprisal from me whatsoever.

"Ribbit!" I yelled and, with a short running start, tackled him in the water. Both of us went down with a splash, but he was the only one surprised by my sudden move.

Well, maybe I was, too. I'd been looking at him for the past two days and wondering, in some human-contact kind of way, what it would be like to touch him. I never thought it would happen unless he tried another stunt like he did at the anniversary party, but here we were and here it was happening.

"You little son of a..." He recovered quickly—too quickly for my taste. I wasn't quite ready for round two yet.

"I've been called more names than I care to

admit." I tried to stand, but the undertow was making it damn difficult. "Many of them unrepeatable." I almost had it. "But I've never been called 'little.'"

I lost. He shouted a short war cry and pounced. My head went under, and I took in my first mouthful of ocean water. Whatever expectations I'd come up with about it, they were entirely blown. This wasn't the slightly chlorine-tasting clear water found in swimming pools across America. It was some of the nastiest, saltiest, most disgusting liquid I'd ever had the displeasure to have in my mouth. It even beat the liquid form of penicillin I was forced to take as a child when I came down with bronchitis every winter. I didn't think anything could beat that...until now.

My head came up, and I spat out all the water I hadn't swallowed. I couldn't see, but I heard him laughing. Not a problem. I reached out in one swift motion and pulled his feet from under him.

Jordan went over backwards, and his audible laugh became a series of bubbles that floated up to the surface.

Even though I had a bit more time to right myself, playing in the ocean was something he'd grown up with and his response time was better than mine. We ended in a face-off, both of us laughing so hard we could barely manage to fight the constant pull from the ocean.

"Truce?" I asked.

"I don't know." He wiped some water off his forehead before it could get into his eyes. "Were we having a moment?"

"If so, you must have had yours in private

underwater," I sniped.

"Well..." He raised an eyebrow. "At least now I know what you'd look like in a wet T-shirt contest."

"Yeah, that's been one of life's biggest unsolved mysteries until now." I had an idea. "At least I'm not the one with the erection now."

A look of panic appeared on his face, and by the time he looked down to confirm what I'd told him, it was too late. I threw myself at him one last time and knocked him back into the water. Unfortunately, he wrapped his arms around my chest, and I was forced to pull him back up again if I wanted to breathe.

"Wow." My voice had grown soft. "You're gullible, too."

"Wow is right," came the reply, just as softly.

If he didn't unwrap himself from my body, one of us would be having a claustrophobic bathing suit in a moment. I don't think that would have bothered him in the least. In fact, he seemed perfectly comfortable with the way our bodies were intertwined.

I don't know if I was comfortable with it or not. Maybe this is what he meant by having a moment, but it was one I couldn't share in his way. In my eyes, Jordan had years of interpreting this kind of closeness in a language I couldn't speak.

Instead of following whatever natural impulses he was feeling, he let me decide the outcome. It meant a great deal to me that he respected me enough to not do something rash and risk the friendship we were building. Whatever he was hoping for, I doubted I could give it to him.

No, I *knew* I wouldn't give it to him because that

wasn't who I was.

He must have seen the confusion on my face and read my resolution because he suddenly released his grip and fell back into the water. I extended my hand, helped him up and together we started back for the car.

※ ※ ※

Neither of us spoke as we dried off, but I think that was because we were busy talking to ourselves. His conversation was one I would rather have been privy to than the one trying to make itself heard in my head. It really sucked that the one person I could identify with and relate to was someone I was...

What? I think that was the part of the conversation I didn't want to explore, and shut the voice out before it could speak any further. Doing that was practically second nature to me now.

It was during the ride home that things really began to become uncomfortable. No matter how I sat or which side of my rear end I favored, it felt like there was sandpaper down there, and it was driving me nuts. To make matters worse, the more I wiggled, however nonchalantly, the more the irritation spread. Before long, it was in the absolute worst area, and that really made me uncomfortable. What the hell was it? A fish? Seaweed? Considering what the water tasted like, there was no telling what the hell was breeding in that water.

"Are you okay?" Jordan glanced over at me.

"I'm fine," I lied.

"You're fine?"

I nodded, but he wasn't satisfied.

"You're practically breakdancing in your

189

swimsuit."

"Breakdancing? That is so early eighties!" I couldn't believe he'd used that reference. "Something feels a bit uncomfortable down there, and I don't know what it is."

"Why didn't you just say something? It's sand." Jordan rolled his eyes. "I guess maybe I should have mentioned it. Anytime you mess around in the ocean like we were, you're going to get some sand in your suit. Since we didn't shower at the beach, you probably wouldn't have noticed you had any down there. Just hop in the tub when we get back to the house."

"Believe me, I'm going to. And, for clarification purposes, we weren't 'messing around.' We were..." Playing with each other? That didn't sound right. Wrestling? Having a good time? It was all too damn suggestive! "We were in the ocean, that's all, and now I have sand up the crack of my ass and it's extremely uncomfortable." At least it was sand and not something living. I was grateful for that. "I just hope I don't need help getting it all out."

"Don't tease."

"I mean medical help, you jackass!" It was my turn to roll the eyes. "I like a good adventure as much as the next person, but that's a little too Indiana Jones for me."

"Exactly how much of an adventure do you really like?" The hint of mischief had reappeared in his voice, and I immediately found myself interested.

"As long we can remain fully clothed in this adventure, run it by me. Otherwise, save yourself some bruises on the arm."

"I was thinking that, since you and I were

talking about gay culture earlier, you might want to go out dancing tonight at a gay club." He almost left it at that but decided to add something else, apparently just in case I misinterpreted him. "If nothing else, you would have the experience at your disposal for your writing." Ah, he was appealing to my sense of the future. "You don't even have to dance if you don't want to."

"Uh..." It was a really wild prospect, and one that was extremely tempting just for the sake of doing it. On the other hand, doing it for that reason alone wasn't reason enough for the sake of practicality. I was trying to grow up and reach out for the person I wanted to be, only I really didn't know who I wanted to be—not anymore, if ever.

That could be part of the problem of why I'd stayed so "in touch with my inner child" and never entirely grown up. Despite not knowing who I did want to be, I knew exactly who I didn't. I didn't want to be a Kay-Mart manager. I had too much ambition and raw energy to settle for a life like that.

But I'd write about it. I wanted to write.

"Okay," I heard myself say.

"You'll go?" Jordan seemed as surprised to hear it as I was to have said it.

"Yeah." I flashed him a warning glance. "But I'm not going to promise I won't dance. I like dancing, so if you're embarrassed by it, then you don't have to hang around with me."

"You might want me to stick close." He seemed a bit more serious than earlier. "You've never been to one of these before, and it can be a little overwhelming, especially in your case. There may be people who come up to you or stare at you or are a little more forward than you're used to. It may get uncomfortable."

"More forward than you?" Was that possible? "I find that a bit difficult to believe. Besides, I can handle myself. I've got a strong sense of wit, a sharp tongue and three years of martial arts training behind me."

"Riiight. Let me know when you get over yourself." It was obvious he didn't believe me. "If anybody does get too close to you, just call them Mary. It should make them back off."

"I told you, I can handle myself."

"Oh, I don't doubt that. With that attitude of yours, I figure you've been handling yourself for years, since you won't let anyone get close enough to do it for you."

"You're really starting to annoy me again." I flashed him a sour look. "Just because I said I'd go to a gay bar with you tonight doesn't mean we're bosom buddies. You don't get to talk about my sex life."

"I'm sorry." He sounded sincere. Again, I was suspicious, and my suspicions were confirmed a moment later. "To be honest, I didn't think you had one." It was the same damn thing I would have said if the situation were reversed.

Actually, I probably deserved that. I had never apologized to him about the other day, and now didn't seem like a good time. Despite this, I didn't feel bad about it. The opportunity would present itself, and Jordan and I were on even ground for the moment. I just hoped to God Jenny and Kenny didn't think the reason I was going out to the bar tonight was because I was gay. And if they had any suspicions or questions, I'd rather they asked me instead of Grandma. I could just imagine what would happen if *she* ever got word of this.

Maybe this wasn't such a good idea after all.

※ ※ ※

The first thing I did after we walked in the door was jump into the shower. I'd never paid so much attention to my rear end in my entire life! It was still pretty raw, but I put some aloe lotion for sunburns down there to soothe it, which created yet another strange sensation. Two in one day. I was on a roll.

I didn't have my entire wardrobe at my disposal, but even if I had, I didn't know if I owned anything appropriate for a gay bar. Maybe that was actually a good thing. Jordan suggested something simple, like shorts and a T-shirt, and luckily that's what I had with me.

He tried several times to lend me a pair of his shorts, but that was just so he could say I'd been in his pants. I might be a little slow, but I wasn't entirely stupid. Besides, it was something I would have pulled.

Jordan was still in the shower, and I was attempting to get some of my clothes together to do a load of wash, when Lenny came into the bedroom with me.

"My mom says you're going out dancing tonight with Jordan."

"That's right." I smiled at him and continued putting my clothes together.

"Do you like dancing?" For a nine-year-old boy, he was extremely direct in asking questions and

193

intent on getting an answer, very much like his mother, I suspected.

"Yes." I put down what was in my hand and gave him my full attention. "I like dancing very much. Do you?"

"No." He eyed me curiously. "Are you going to bring home a boyfriend?"

"Not unless hell freezes over or somebody drugs me." Where was he getting these questions from? Was this stuff talked about in the schools here? "Why would you think I'd bring somebody home after dancing?"

"I heard Aunt Diane on the phone tonight and she said you're a closet case."

"I don't know what makes your aunt Diane tick, but I hope it's a time bomb." I'd better watch what I was saying. Kids had the most unpleasant habit of repeating everything they heard, and it was almost always to the wrong people. Case in point. "I was just joking about that. I'm sure your aunt Diane only made a passing comment and she didn't mean to sound like such a bi—" Oh, that would have been lovely to explain. First I want the woman to blow up and then I call her a bitch. Why not just tell him what I was really thinking? "...insensitive person."

"Do you like men? Aunt Diane said she thinks you do, but you just don't know it." He paused. "It's that or you're a cong...cong..." It was obvious he was trying very hard to come up with the word.

"Congenial? As in friendly? Social?"

He shook his head.

"Congested?" What was it? What had the witch said about me?

"Congenital idiot!" he announced triumphantly.

"Well, isn't that special?" Diane thought I was either gay or an idiot. At least she was willing to give me the benefit of the doubt, which is more than I can say for any number of other people throughout the years. "Do you believe everything you hear?" The absurdity of that question hit me. "Look who I'm asking. A nine-year-old boy. You'd believe me if I told you the Teenage Mutant Ninja Turtles were out in your living room." I couldn't believe this. "I'm starting to feel a bit stressed." I buried my head in my hands.

"Want me to make you a martini?"

"Excuse me?" I looked at him. "Make me a *what?*"

"Whenever my mom or dad feels stressed, I make them a martini or sometimes a mint julep." He could tell by the look on my face that I found it difficult to believe a word he said. "Don't you believe me?" I shook my head. "You put a few ice cubes into a mixer, then three things of gin and one tiny thing of vermouth. Stir until the cubes start to melt and then pour into a cold glass. Just before I give it to them, I add a piece of lemon or an olive, unless I'm making a gibson, then I add one of those small onions." My mouth must have been wide open. "Do you want me to tell you how to make a mint julep?"

"No, I'm...sure you know what you're doing." Hell, *I* didn't even know how to make one. "In fact, it scares me no end that you know what you're doing. I thought you were fibbing at first, telling me a little white lie."

"There's no such thing as a little white lie!" he chastised me. "Besides, I don't have to lie like grownups do."

"You're a child. Children specialize in lying." I put my hand on his shoulder. "I know this, see, because I was one once." I didn't have a brother to blame things on like he did, though. "Later on in life, some of us get in touch with our inner child and start lying all over again. Fortunately, like yourself, I don't lie, either."

"Aunt Diane said you're still lying—to yourself. She said you're dying to become a sex donkey."

"Excuse me?" Did Jenny know what influence her friend was having on these children? Oh, hell, they already knew how to make two different kinds of martinis, so how much worse could it be? "Please, don't use words like that. It's really not good for someone your age to say them."

"Sorry." He frowned and tried to rearrange words in his head. "She says you're dying to..."

"*I get the point!*" This kid knew far too much about things I certainly never knew about at his age. He was also one heck of an eavesdropper. "Where did you ever hear words like those, anyway? Not just from your mom and aunt, I hope." I know for damn sure he never heard it from my great-aunt and uncle.

"This is California," he told me matter-of-factly.

"Oh, good." I stared at him. "So, you're familiar with the term *precocious*?"

"You use a word like *precocious* on a nine-year-old?" There was something odd I couldn't quite identify in his voice. "How pretentious."

"Maybe," I tried to laugh it off, "but can you spell it?"

"Can *you*?"

"Um..." My smirk faded as I realized the little bastard had me. "I have to get ready."

❀ ❀ ❀

"Hey!" Jordan poked his head around the doorjamb. "You almost ready?"

I was lying down on the bed trying to invoke some kind of meditation. For the past half-hour, I'd almost expected someone from *Candid Camera* to come jumping out telling me what a fantastic joke had been played on me, or that I'd hear Rod Serling's voice speaking to an audience about my trip into the Twilight Zone.

Why did it feel like walls were closing in around me? Maybe they always had been, it was only now that I could see them. They weren't clear yet, but I knew they were there. Why couldn't I see them for what they were? Why was it so difficult? Was I just being stubborn or was it reality not wanting me to see the complete picture yet?

"Yeah." I sat up and swung my legs over the side. "For better or worse, I'm ready and raring to go."

"You have a scowl on your face."

"I think I'm just a little nervous." I tried to sound a little more together than I actually was. "I feel like...Do you remember that movie *The Black Hole?*" He nodded. "It's like I'm in this nice little self-contained ship, which is my sphere of experience, and I'm staring into something completely unknown to me. I don't like the unknown because it's not always a safe bet.

"That's the only time I ever gamble, which tells you how often I do it. I actually feel more comfortable with repetition then I do taking an actual risk. Take tonight, for instance. Even though

197

it's just dancing..."

He was eyeing me closely now, probably trying to figure out if I was going to tell him I'd changed my mind.

"Small experiences, the smallest, can make a difference in a person's life. Once they've had that experience, they're changed forever. Change doesn't bother me when I know what to expect—and you were right earlier. I have no idea what to expect, and that scares me, but I don't want to stay home. I do want to go. Something tells me I *have* to go."

"You aren't going to tell me that you had a mystical experience, are you?" Jordan smirked. "There weren't any imaginary people who came to you while I was in the shower and told you to do this tonight, were there? You don't hear voices, do you?"

"I didn't mention that when I get that scared feeling in the pit of my stomach, I start taking my aggressions out on anyone around me, did I? If not, then I also probably didn't mention that—"

"I get the point. I just haven't learned when you want to be taken seriously, and...when you're attempting foreplay."

I lunged off the bed, but he had already taken off running for the kitchen. When I finally caught up to him, he had positioned himself with Jenny between us. That was okay. He'd pay! Sometimes the anticipation was worse than the actual act of revenge. *And after I'm done with you...*

Jordan moved out into the open, knowing full well that I wouldn't do anything with someone else around; and I took in my first full look at him. I didn't know whether to whimper or just put a bag over my head. As one masculine guy comfortable with his heterosexuality giving another guy a compliment, he looked damn near perfect.

Maybe I was putting him on too much of a pedestal, but I really had nothing to gain by stating exactly how he came across. It wasn't like he was going to hear my thoughts and I'd then be rewarded by another kiss or something else even more unsavory.

He was wearing a white T-shirt, which accentuated his chest more than any shirt I'd seen him in so far, and a pair of shorts that, while not sleazy or faggy, definitely broadcast sex-appeal. I had a feeling it was going to be a very long night.

"Now, Jordan." Jenny handed him a sheet of paper. "This is the number of the hotel we'll be staying at, and the club where the reception is being held. Don't worry about the kids. Diane is taking them for the night, so you don't have to be in early, and she's also taking them to practice tomorrow. That frees you up in case you two decide to go to the beach in the afternoon."

"Are you and Kenny going somewhere?" No one had mentioned a thing about them having plans for anything. I just hoped I wasn't interrupting or overstaying my welcome. "If you need to drop me back off with Grandma, that's fine. I don't want to get in the way."

"Oh, good grief!" Jenny laughed. "You're not in the way at all, Andy. Kenny and I have this wedding to go to, and Diane was going to take the kids anyway to give Jordan the night off. Besides, I'm glad you'll be here to keep him in line." She gave him a mischievous look. "Now I don't have to worry about the neighbors complaining about any strange noises coming from the house."

"Strange noises?" What was she talking about? "I don't make a lot of noise," I informed them, and they both stared at me.

Oh, those kinds of noises.

"Well, sure, I mean I'll rock the house." That still didn't sound so good. "Just not tonight. I'll be quiet tonight." That didn't help. "Because nothing is going to happen tonight. Why don't I just shut up now."

"Right. I have to go get dressed, then Kenny and I will drop Lenny and Benny off. You two have fun tonight, but not too much fun!" Again came the mischievous look.

"For crying out loud, Jenny, we're just going dancing and maybe grab a queer…"

They both looked at me.

"Beer. Grab a beer." I shook my head. "Well, I can see how this night is starting out."

8

Jordan and I left a short time later. There wasn't much conversation in the vehicle, but that was probably my fault. I was afraid to open my mouth in case something stupid came out again—another Freudian slip or worse.

There was so much around me that had to do with homosexuality that it was no wonder it was on my mind. It was probably the only time in adulthood that a heterosexual could say it was healthy for homosexuality to be on his mind—there was no way to avoid it in this particular area of the state.

I almost wished for the by-the-numbers existence back in Michigan at Kay-Mart, home and school. Maybe vacations weren't what they were made out to be. Maybe I'd just explore part of my own state next time. Then, too, maybe I was doing it all wrong. Most of the people I knew were going out of the *country*, so maybe that was the way to go. Change should be in moderation, not the complete utter chaos of culture shock I'd experienced so far.

My own quote came back to me. The smallest experience can make a difference in a person's life. Once they've had it, they're changed forever. I didn't want these experiences! I didn't ask for them, and I had the choice to decide how much I was going to let them become a part of me.

There was too much at risk to back out of going to the club tonight. I had to prove to myself that I was capable of getting through it without being manipulated.

By the time we arrived at the club, I'd worked myself up into an attitude I was sure would keep everybody at a certain distance from me. If they ignored the nonverbal communication I was giving off, God help them, because I wasn't in the mood to be nice. Mr. Nice Guy was no more.

"Try to stay around the dance floor and bar," Jordan told me before getting out of the car. "There's a lounge area, but avoid it if you can because that's where most of the people looking to hook up for the night hang out. If you're approached, and I'm quite sure you will be, don't show any hesitation in telling them you aren't interested. If things get really rough, just remember to say 'Mary.'" He turned to me and grinned. "I don't want to have to rescue you."

"Don't worry about me. The last time somebody tried to pick me up, I was still in diapers." I climbed out, shut the door and waited patiently for him to lead the way.

"You know," he called out to me, "underneath that callous and self-defeating attitude of yours is a very handsome and attractive young man."

"Jordan, I look like I just stepped out of a GQ

magazine and fell flat on my face." I sighed. "People look at you and think you're an angel. They look at me and think I'm a Saint...Bernard."

He locked the car and gave me a strange side-long look before starting for the entrance.

Inside was nothing short of spectacular. There was a short corridor lit in blue neon lights where one paid the cover charge, checked a coat if there was one and then moved on into the club. A large bar lined with green neon lights took up the entire right side of the room, while the dance floor took up the remaining space. The walls were decorated in various other fluorescent colors while a number of moving lights, strobes and laser lights practically turned the dance floor into a set from a science fiction movie.

And the music! It was the perfect mix of dance and club all blended together in a continuous feast for the ears. I could easily get used to a place like this.

Beyond the dance floor, way in the back, was an opening that appeared to lead into what must have been the lounge Jordan warned me about. If it wasn't for the fact I had to use the bathroom, I probably could have avoided that area the entire night. Unfortunately, having worked myself up into such a frenzy in the car, I really had to go now.

All I really wanted to do was get a beer and go stand in some dark corner, listen to the music, watch those around me and maybe dance a lone dance or two. It didn't qualify as blending in, but this was officially research.

I made my way through a few clusters of people, mostly guys, and finally reached the archway that separated the lounge from the rest of the floor. Of course, it couldn't be clear of traffic and give me a quick shot in and out. Nooo. That would be too much to ask for. Instead, the entire wall beyond the opening was lined with every age, color and race known to man, all of them gay, all of them looking, all of them making me very nervous. All I had to survive this were my wit and my legs.

"Hey, there."

I looked up and saw a man, probably in his forties, looking me up and down. I think this officially passed as being "checked out." There was nothing really distinguishing about him except for some gray hair in his moustache and neatly trimmed beard—and maybe the loose silk shirt he had on. If nothing else, the man had fashion sense.

Wasn't there some stereotype about gay men being keenly aware of fashion and all the latest styles? If that's the case, then I sure as hell could never be gay. It's jeans and T-shirts for me until I die.

"Hello." I felt really strange responding, mostly because this was the first conversation I'd ever had with an older gay man. What did they talk about? Would it be anything I could relate to, or was I going to have to fake my way through it like I had sports at the anniversary party?

"I know you from somewhere, don't I?" He raised his hand and held his chin as if in deep thought. "Were you out at the park the last couple of nights?"

"Park? What park?" All the parks in LA, and I was supposed to know exactly which one he was talking about? "And what would I be doing at this park?"

"Griffith Park." He licked his lips. "Looking for some action."

I shook my head. He peered at me even harder.

"I'd swear I've seen you somewhere before...and it had to be recently. Have we ever...?"

"I'm straight," I informed him. That solved that little trick of his memory and saved me from having to hear whatever it is he'd done with someone who either looked like or reminded him of me.

"Then we haven't...?"

"Oh, no!" Mama always told me there'd be days like these. Not really, but I'm sure if she knew where I was, she would have warned me appropriately. "No, no, no, no...I could never...not even if I was intox—" I was babbling. "I'm definitely straight. In fact, I am so straight that even straight people question how straight they are when they're around me because I give off such a strong straight vibe. It–It causes a lot of problems."

My talking like this caused a lot of problems. I was nervous, sweating profusely and still hadn't made it to the damn bathroom.

"Well..." He winked. "...your loss."

"Right." I hurried away. Whatever.

Finally, I made it to the bathroom! Unfortunately, I'd barely made it through the door when another guy came up to me. Didn't they ever quit? Didn't they know the look in a man's eye that boldly tells them to stay the hell away from him until he's peed? Why couldn't he just *get out of my way*?

At least Jordan had warned me ahead of time to expect people to do this. Well, maybe not interrupting me going to the bathroom, but certainly coming up to me. I'd have to remember to thank him for that.

"What are you looking for?" he asked, doing the same checking-me-out routine the last guy did.

"The toilet," I replied, somewhat impatient.

"The toilet?" He looked perplexed, like I was speaking a foreign language.

"The toilet." I told him again. It wasn't that difficult of a concept to grasp. "The john, the can, the crapper, the potty, the throne, the urinal, the pisspot—all of which you are blocking me from getting to!"

"No." He sighed. "I meant what are you *looking* for?"

"Looking for?" I asked through clenched teeth. "What did I lose?" What did he *think* I was looking for? I'd just told him! Considering where we were, chances are I was looking to get rid of something, not pick something up.

"Lose? Huh?" His state of confusion didn't improve. Realization hadn't dawned on him yet, if it ever would.

"Well, you obviously know something I don't." I shrugged and looked at him expectantly. "Tell me what I've lost, and I'll tell you what I'm looking for. In the meantime..." I moved around him. "...I'll be over here relieving myself at whatever it is you call it in whatever little world you live in."

I didn't care where he went or what he did as long as I finally got to pee in peace!

There were three urinals on the left and three stalls on the right. All the doors on the stalls were closed, and the only open urinal was in the middle.

206

As a rule, I always use an end one because that way I have at least some privacy on one side of me. Since I had to go so bad, though, I wasn't about to be fussy. I just walked up, looked right in front of me at the wall, undid what I needed to undo, freed what I needed to free and started doing what I needed so desperately to do—and did it feel fantastic.

Several satisfying seconds later, I began to notice a strange sound coming from behind me in one of the stalls. There was a rhythmic thumping accompanied by an occasional gasp. Either somebody was having a heart attack or there were two people in there doing the nasty.

Oh, come on! In a bathroom stall? That is *so* tacky.

Despite that, I couldn't help chuckling. Then, out of the corner of my eye, I saw the guy on my right staring at me. I hoped he didn't think I was chuckling because I was doing something other than relieving myself. That *really* would have been tacky.

"Nice," he muttered.

"What?" I looked over at him, something I'd been trying to avoid, and found him staring down at my...

Well, he was staring down at me. I'd thought he might have been commenting on the commotion in the stall, but apparently he was critiquing my...

He was critiquing it.

"I said..." He finally looked up at my face. "...it's nice."

"Thank you?" I mean, what the hell was I supposed to say? Why couldn't this have happened in one of those bizarre dreams I'd been having instead of reality?

This place was a nightmare! Guys going at it in a bathroom stall, guys checking other guys' privates out at the urinals...Was this normal? I mean, for crying out loud, I'd certainly never heard of these things going on in a *straight* bar.

Just when I thought things couldn't possibly get any worse, the man who'd thought he recognized me burst into the bathroom. It only took a few seconds for him to zero in on me, and then he made his announcement.

"You!" He pointed me out to everyone. "You're that pop star who did the striptease at the Ambassador the other night!"

Heads suddenly turned towards me. Even the thudding and gasping coming from the stall paused.

"You've got the most incredible ass I've ever seen!"

Stall doors unlocked, and pairs of heads peered out to catch a glimpse of who this moron was talking about.

Me!

"You must have me confused with someone else," I stammered and zipped everything back up, "because I have no idea what you're talking about."

How in the hell had this guy seen me at the Ambassador? It wasn't a gay club, was it? Oh, God, what if it was? Hadn't Jenny said something about sugar daddies? Actually, that would explain why the group of girls who approached us on the beach earlier didn't show any interest in me other than admiring my ass. Hell, I hadn't even gotten a phone number out of it.

Yep, they were gay.

"His ass?" The guy next to me spoke up. "You should see his—"

"Shut up!" Jordan had said something similar to me earlier today, and I really didn't need to hear it again.

Speaking of that twit, I wished he was here to rescue me, but then he'd never let me live it down, especially after I made such a fuss about being able to take care of myself. Still, I had to admit that seeing him now would be a relief.

"Dude," one of the guys peeking out of a stall called out to me, "I've got, like, all your albums!"

"Ignore him." Another voice rang out. "Why don't you come in here, and the two of us can make some music of our own?"

"I am so out of here." I all but ran out of that bathroom.

The guy who had come in after me gave me a look as I was leaving that told me he understood my discomfort at being in this situation but didn't really care. I'd never seen that kind of look in a man's eye before, and I didn't like it. I felt like I was an object instead of a human being, like a waitress at Hooters.

The DJ was playing Dead Or Alive's "Brand New Lover" when I stepped back out into the main area of the club. There were too many people dancing to even hope to find Jordan anytime soon. As much as I'd wanted distance between us since we'd met, I would have felt safer if I could at least have been within shouting distance of him, especially after the incident in the bathroom.

I really had been a prick to him. He didn't deserve my attitude or my prying questions, yet he took them both in stride. He teased me quite a bit but never made me feel like the guy who recognized me from the Ambassador had just done. Jordan really wasn't so bad.

The smallest experiences...

All this time I'd been thinking I was too good to know him, too good to be friends with a homosexual; and maybe it was really the other way around. Here I was in a gay club, surrounded by gay men and women, and bathrooms aside, it actually seemed safer and more fun than regular heterosexual clubs. There were a few people making out here and there, but not doing anything completely outrageous.

Of course, getting used to seeing guys kissing other guys and women kissing other women took a little getting used to. There weren't any drugs, that I could see, being sold and used. There weren't any racial fights breaking out over who had the right to frequent the club or battles for the favor of a partner. There were just people dancing with their boyfriends, girlfriends or just friends and having a good time.

Somewhere in the center of all this was Jordan. He was the eye of the hurricane, the one who had made sense of all of this some time ago, and I was caught up in the swirl of what society wanted me to believe versus what I saw with my own eyes. The people I was watching didn't resemble the ones from the bathroom in any way at all. Everything was in conflict with everything else, but I was beginning to see beyond some of the lies, and it

210

scared the hell out of me.

I felt certain Jordan could help explain why. At least, I hoped so, because I just wasn't sorting it out on my own.

I turned to search the crowd on my left and saw a decent-looking light-haired kid about my age approaching me.

"Would you like a blowjob?" he asked goodnaturedly.

"Excuse me?" I stared at him, exasperated. These people had no shame at all. Maybe I was wrong about being wrong about them. Maybe they *were* like the ones in the bathroom. "I thought only the guys in that back area asked questions like that."

"What?" He looked perplexed. "Oh, that." He actually blushed, which took me by surprise. For whatever twisted reason, he seemed sincere. "I was talking about the drink. That kid over there said it was your favorite."

I looked to see which kid he was talking about and discovered Jordan watching me and grinning from ear to ear. All the nice things I'd been thinking about him vanished. He'd pay.

"I saw the two of you come in together. It didn't look like he was your boyfriend, so I asked him what your name was and if it would be okay if I bought you a drink. My name's Nate."

"Hello, Nate." I extended my hand, and he shook it. "I'm Andy and that rotten little son of a..." I collected my cool. "That kid over there is Jordan. Forgive him. He has issues and comes from a family that thinks Beethoven's *Fifth* is a quantity of liquor. Now, to answer your original question, no,

211

thank you."

"Oh." He looked a little bit dejected. "Well..."

"However, if they have it, a shot of Jungle Juice sounds good." He perked back up. "I'll pay for it, though." I might as well set the ground rules right now. If he thought because he was going to pay for the drinks he was entitled to something on the side later on...

"You don't have to. I'm not looking for anything other than conversation."

Well, this was a first so far tonight.

"It's just that I saw you come in, and I really wanted to meet you and..." He paused. "You look really nervous. Is this your first time in a place like this?"

"Nervous? What makes you think I'm nervous?" A stream of sweat ran from my forehead down to my cheek. "Yeah, actually, it is my first time. Here. It's my first time here, as in, a place like this." And I had Jordan to thank for it. "I guess I've never been into the whole male bondage thing."

"You mean male bonding?"

"Whatever." I had to stop dwelling on Jordan. "By chance, do you wear contacts? Not many people come up to me, even if it's just for conversation."

"No, I don't. I used to say the same thing to myself when I first came out and people would come up to me and tell me they were interested. It got a lot worse when I found out they only wanted sex and didn't care who I was as a person.

"I didn't feel very handsome to begin with, and I felt even uglier then, like I was only good enough for a one-night stand and not a long-term relationship. They were wrong, though, and so was

I."

Nate was hitting on fears that a lot of people, gay or straight, have felt at one time or another.

"That's why I promised myself I would never approach someone unless I'm attracted to them and willing to get to know them for who they are."

"Wow! That's really sweet." I was practically melting. Actually, it reminded me of everything I was feeling the night I met Jordan, except there wasn't any alcohol involved this time. I wondered if it really had been the champagne after all. "I appreciate you telling me that..."

Wait a moment. Had he just said in a round-about way that he was attracted to me? He never approached someone unless he was attracted to them and was willing to get to know them for who they were. Let's see...he'd offered me a drink and was making conversation. Yep, that probably constituted some kind of attraction.

"...but I think it's only fair to tell you that I'm straight."

"Fair enough." His composure didn't change in the slightest, which surprised me yet again. "That means we can still talk and dance, though, doesn't it?"

"Absolutely. Straight people do those things, too, you know?" I looked over at Jordan again and watched him for a moment. It was obvious he was wondering what was going on over here, if anything. I flipped him off. "Tell you what. Why don't we skip the drink for now and go dance? In fact, why don't we go out there and make Jordan wish he was a member of the female gender." I pulled Nate out onto the floor with me.

"He won't be the only one."

♣ ♣ ♣

The beginning of the middle of my evening played out an awful lot like the end of an episode of *The Love Boat*. I couldn't remember a night when the company was better, the music more melodic or when I'd been happier. I didn't dance as a hetero- or homosexual or with any specific label attached, nor did anyone else. We all just danced.

Hell, even I was surprised by my ability to adapt and fit in without making everyone around me desire my head on a platter due to my abrasive and often ignorant manner.

Nate turned out to be a man of his word and didn't make a single move on me. I was pretty sure he wanted to, but he respected what I'd told him about being straight. Of course, this lasted only for the first five minutes he and I were out on the dance floor. Things got a little complicated after that.

I don't think Jordan appreciated being flipped off, mostly because I don't think he expected that I would go out and dance with Nate. He would have found it amusing if I had overreacted or gone running back to his side, but it didn't work out that way and it probably irritated him. I found that to be extremely amusing. *Paybacks are a bitch, J-man!* He'd be so jealous of the fact I could have a great time in somebody else's arms that...

I don't know what else, but damn it he'd be jealous...and miserable!

"Your friend seems to be having a really good time, too," Nate shouted over the music.

"What?" I turned to where he was looking and

saw Jordan dancing with some ugly guy. To make matters worse, he really did appear to be enjoying himself. *You bastard! This wasn't supposed to be happening like this.* He was supposed to be miserable, not happy.

Jordan caught my gaze, and a grin of pure, irritating satisfaction appeared on his face. He must have thought he was getting the response out of me that he was intending. Ha! I'd show him. I wasn't the miserable one.

"Uh-oh." Nate's voice sounded louder than it had before, and I realized the music had stopped.

Unfortunately, I'd been so wrapped up in watching Jordan acting like he was happy I hadn't noticed, and continued right on dancing. I stopped.

"I think they're going to play a slow song," he said.

"What's the matter?" It was too perfect. Anyone can fast dance with a partner, but slow dancing? It required one to be right up against another in a much more intimate fashion. Jordan would be miserable watching this for sure, and then he'd have to leave me alone because he'd know once and for all that I wasn't the least bit interested in him. "Can't you slow dance?"

"Yeah, of course." The first few chords of Roxette's "Listen To Your Heart" sounded. "I just didn't think you'd be comfortable..."

"Get over here." I pulled him closer. There was no time for this nonsense about whether or not I was comfortable. Screw that.

He wrapped his arms around my waist, I put mine around his, and we started moving to the music. There!

Now that everything was as it should be, I allowed myself to relax a moment and take in the changes around me. Nate was wearing very pleasant cologne, but I couldn't place it. One thing for sure is that it was probably a lot more expensive then the stuff I had, the same stuff I forgot to put on before I left. He was sweating a bit, too, and the ends of his hair were damp, reminding me a bit of how Corey Hart looked in one of his videos.

Actually, I don't know which one of us was giving off heat, but I was starting to sweat again just by being so close to him. His body felt nice, though, so nice that I just went ahead and rested my chin on his shoulder. Nate didn't seem to mind at all, and I was glad he was comfortable with a straight boy being able to do that without him reading anything into it.

"You smell nice," he murmured in my ear. "What are you wearing?"

"Irish Spring, I think."

"It's Dove." A familiar voice whispered in my other ear. How in the world could he have heard Nate's question over the music?

I nonchalantly turned Nate around so I could glare at my tormentor. Jordan was slow-dancing next to us—*right* next to us—with Dog Man. He wasn't satisfied with just their hands being around each other's waists. No, he had to have his hands on the other guy's shoulders while the canine crossbreed was running his hands along Jordan's back.

I pulled Nate even closer, and raised my eyebrow at Jordan. Two could play at this game.

He moved close enough to talk again.

"You really shouldn't flip people off like that." He rested his chin on his partner's shoulder, mimicking my pose. "They're liable to take it the wrong way."

"Really?" I asked in mock exaggeration. "I thought it was pretty self-explanatory."

"Yeah, but..." He peered at me. "...you shouldn't make promises you aren't willing to keep."

The mutt suddenly moved them off a bit and gave us some room. Why did I get the feeling Jordan thought he'd just gotten away with something? So I had flipped him off—big deal. Maybe it was another one of those California things.

"What was all that about?" Nate wanted to know. It was stupid of me to think he hadn't heard the exchange.

"Nate." I picked my head up off of his shoulder and looked directly at him. "What does it mean when you flip somebody off?"

"It means 'fuck you.'"

"That's what I thought." I sighed in relief. Is that how Jordan saw it, though? If I flip him off, he's probably going to say I was giving him some hidden message, but what was the message? *Don't make promises you aren't willing to keep.* "So, he thinks I'm telling him I want to..." My face dropped. "That asshole!"

"I don't get this." Nate stopped dancing and stared at me, a frown on his face. "You say you're straight, yet you're so preoccupied with your friend that you aren't paying attention to anything or anyone else. What do you care how he takes you flipping him off? Why let it bother you? And why do you care who he's dancing with?"

I was caught off-guard by his questions, and he picked up on it right away.

"I'd have to be pretty blind not to notice that you haven't been able to stop watching them since I mentioned they were out on the dance floor. Are you attracted to this friend of yours or something?"

"Oh, please." I rolled my eyes. "I'd like to think I have some semblance of taste. Besides, Jordan's best quality is his absence. I can't stand his looks, and his personality is...well..."

"He's been watching you, too," Nate said.

"Really?" I asked—a little too quickly.

Nate gave me a sad look and shook his head.

"I'm sorry." I hadn't realized how rude I was being. "You're right. I shouldn't care what he says or who he's with. It's none of my business, and I *have* been ignoring you, which isn't what I meant to do at all." My words appeared to be finding their mark. "Why don't we just forget about all this, keep dancing and have ourselves a good time?"

I know he wanted to make me feel a bit worse for having neglected him because I could see his hesitation, but he finally gave in, sighed and pulled me close to finish the dance.

This was the sort of thing that always used to happen to me in the past. I'd ask a girl to dance, and she'd stare at some other guy all night. Now I was the one doing it, and that made me feel like a total jerk. When and how had the roles reversed without my realizing it, and when the hell had I become so irresistible?

I sneaked a glance Jordan's way when we turned, and it appeared his dancing partner was giving him shit, too. Actually, neither of us had to put up with this. If we were so concerned about what the other was doing, why didn't we just dance together? Maybe that would make things too simple, and after all, Nate wasn't such a bad guy. He was smart, patient and, based on the short amount of time I'd known him, sensitive about my situation. Why, then, was I still thinking about Jordan? Because I was being stupid, that's why.

As soon as the ballad ended and Kon Kan's "I Beg Your Pardon" started up, the floor was instantly packed with sweating bodies moving and gyrating in ways I'd never seen before, not even on *Dance Fever* when I was younger. This was something new, something not choreographed or put on for show or anything like that.

Maybe it was freedom. These people had a knowledge of themselves that I didn't, and they were free to express it any way they wanted. I didn't have that. I had nothing to really express because I didn't have a clue who I was—not anymore.

No, that wasn't true. I did have something to express. I had questions.

❧ ❧ ❧

Nate and I spent the next two and a half hours dancing, talking and drinking. I only had Pepsi after a single shot of Jungle Juice. There was no way I was going to make an ass out of myself and not remember it in the morning.

Besides, Nate really was a great guy and quite handsome, too, but he just wasn't doing anything for me. I didn't expect that he *would* do anything for me, but every time I looked at his face I kept hoping it would be someone else's. Was it because

219

that person did something for me, or was it because it would be a familiar face in a foreign place? Did it really matter?

Actually, yes, it did, and that someone else finally found me sitting at a table when Nate was up getting a refill.

"Are you having a good time?" Jordan asked me. He was going to great pains to seem only mildly interested in my response.

"Lovely." I looked up at him and responded in the same tone. "Couldn't be better." Why was it, again, that I was so glad to see him? The reason was fading…like my patience.

"Glad to hear it." He forced a smile. Yeah, he was believable—not.

"You?" This was more annoying than pleasant, but I'd play along.

"Wonderful!"

"Fabulous!" Two could play at this.

"Where's your friend?" Jordan looked up towards the bar. "Getting another drink?"

I could tell he was struggling with whether or not he should continue the thought because he had the look on his face that most constipated people have—or at least, the actors have on the laxative commercials that dramatized more than was really necessary. The urge to force it out was there, but how much pain it was going to cause was uncertain.

"Getting some napkins to mop up the drool from his mouth and your shirt, maybe?"

So, that's how it was going to be.

"Aren't you charming as always? And where's your…" How could I put this in terms that he could

220

understand? "...whatever it is you call him? Outside barking at the moon or chasing passing cars?"

"We could go outside and look." He motioned towards the door. "Besides, I'm about ready to call it a night. If you don't *mind*, of course."

There was no reason for him to be snide about it. He didn't want to go there with me.

"You can call it whatever you want." I faked the best happy face and civil manner I could just to annoy him. "But I *would* like to say goodbye to Nate."

Jordan declined to make any further comments. When Nate came back, I explained that my friend was leaving and, since he was my ride, that meant I had to take off, too. Nate wasn't very happy about it, but he was gracious, and I even gave him a quick hug. I was glad he didn't give me his address and phone number or ask for mine. I doubted either of us would be getting to each other's state anytime soon, and what would we say to each other even if we did?

Somehow, I got the impression he knew all this, too, but I still couldn't help feeling like I was a jerk. After all, he'd put up with me during the evening, and I'd only given him a hug. Boy, that was big of me. Miss Manners would *not* be pleased.

❧ ❧ ❧

All I could think about on the way back out to the car was how much I wanted to go home, crawl in bed and pull the covers over my head. Since when did I start feeling so confused about life, about myself—and about Jordan? One minute I wanted to apologize to him for being such a jerk and the next I wanted to make him miserable and jealous.

Nate had really turned my night around after the incident in the bathroom and made me question society's beliefs about gays even more than I had before. I had so many questions that had to be answered before I returned to the humdrum life I'd left behind in Michigan. Unfortunately, there wasn't much time, and as much as I still didn't want to admit it, I needed Jordan's help answering them.

"Jordan, I'm—" I started, but was cut off by another voice.

"Jordan!"

We both looked up to see who had called his name. A guy—dare I call him that?—was walking towards us. He was probably a year or two older than Jordan, about a foot taller, built like a brick shithouse, had a stud in his left ear, two hoops in his right, wore a large cowboy hat and carried himself like he was God's gift to homosexuals. I didn't find him particularly attractive—maybe a bit more than Jordan's dancing partner in the club, though I'm sure he'd be the belle of the ball in a prison block.

"JR," Jordan acknowledged. There was a definite coldness in his tone, and I was curious why.

"It's been a while." JR looked him over appreciatively. He had a Southern accent, probably Texan. Well, I thought it might be Texan because of his name, which was straight out of the TV series *Dallas*. "A year at least, right?"

Jordan agreed.

"You still look as good as you did then, maybe better."

I didn't particularly like the way JR was undressing Jordan in his mind and going through a number of sexual fantasies without his consent.

"I've wondered how we keep missing each other at the clubs."

"Luck, I guess."

"Oh..." He grinned arrogantly. "...I can't believe you still have hard feelings. We had some really good times." JR looked around and then motioned back toward his car. "Why don't you get rid of the twig and let's go relive some old memories."

Twig?

"I mean..." He glanced at me again. "...how desperate are you these days?"

I tensed up and sensed Jordan tensing up, too. This was a complication I really didn't need. It was, to say the least, very inconvenient. There was obviously some history between them, and it wasn't entirely pleasant, at least, for one of them. It wasn't difficult to figure out that they'd had sex.

I understood why JR was attracted to Jordan, though I couldn't figure out what Jordan saw in this inspiration for the creature in *Pumpkinhead*. What was that name Jordan told me to call people who were annoying me?

"Why don't you leave him alone, Marie." I finally decided to speak up. After all, the dick had called me a twig.

"Marie?" JR frowned.

"Mary," Jordan leaned over and whispered in my ear.

"Mary," I corrected myself. "Why don't you leave him alone, Mary!"

"Why don't you get lost, Pee-Wee, before I have to take you over my knee, spank you and send you on your way crying for Mommy."

That did it!

"Why don't you go head South for the border, you down-home-on-the-farm, Bob-Evans-eating, sister-molesting, sheep-rearing, bull's-horn-up-your-ass-riding byproduct of a lesbian clusterfuck!"

Jordan did a double-take, and JR's mouth dropped open.

"Now, if you'll excuse us." I put my arm around Jordan and pulled him close. "I'm going to take this hot Adonis home and do something that will make him forget you ever existed, bitch."

It was a safe assumption that JR could have whipped my ass without too much difficulty, but he was too shocked to bother lifting a finger.

I had steered Jordan to the car and locked all the doors before he snapped out of it. He was in a state of shock as well, but not so much that he didn't know not to stick around the parking lot any longer than we had to. We were on our way back home moments later.

❀ ❀ ❀

"I still can't believe you said that to him." Jordan unlocked the back door and let us in. The house was dark, which made sense since we were the only ones there. "That was great!" He flipped on the lights and then looked directly at me. "Nobody's ever stuck up for me like that before." It was the first time I think I'd seen him this sincere and almost at a loss for words. "Thank you."

"I didn't do it for you." I was so angry I was shaking. "He insulted me, and I lost my temper."

Jordan turned away and lowered his head, which pissed me off all the more.

"I can't believe you had sex with that asshole! I

mean, what the hell were you thinking?" I didn't give him a chance to respond. "You could do so much better. At least you know what you're looking for, and you're not afraid of go out and find it, but next time, find something human."

I stopped and tried to calm down. This wasn't the time to berate him. I'd already done plenty of that during the last few days. I needed to find some way to tell him that I actually admired him.

"People don't have to guess with you. It's not at all like that with me. I can just imagine what your aunt thinks about me right now, and it sure wasn't helped by that...friend of hers who seems to think I'm a closet sex donkey sodomite wannabe."

"You want to sodomize a donkey?" He turned to me and made a feeble attempt at humor. It was either that, or he wanted to change the subject.

"Don't fuck with me right now. I'm trying to be serious."

"Well, didn't you ever make a mistake?" Jordan started losing *his* temper, though his eyes were a bit glossy. "Out of all those women you bragged to me that you've been with, never a mistake?" He fought to regain his composure. "How about when you were younger and only had guy friends who stayed overnight? Did you ever get curious? Anyone ever tell on you? Come on," he pleaded, "level with me. Did you ever experiment with any of your friends when you were a kid?"

"Sure. There was Jimmy, Andrew, Mike, Scott, Randy, Rob, Keith and Craig."

He seemed dumbfounded at the number of people on my list. Apparently, he hadn't expected me to be that honest with him. In any case, it took several long moments before he could put his thoughts into words and respond.

"And it never occurred to you that you might be gay?"

"No." It hadn't, really. "Should it have?"

"Who *are* you?" Jordan looked at me like I was one of those pod people from *Invasion of the Body Snatchers*. I might look and talk like Andy, but I definitely wasn't the Andy he'd come to know.

Little did he know that he was hitting on a question I'd been struggling with for a long time now. However, I'd been putting off answering that question for a long time, too.

I'd flirted with an answer once or twice, but never seriously. Part of me desperately wanted to find out and finally come to some resolution, while another part of me fought that course of action with everything it had. That's why I was in turmoil, and that's why I could never be happy with myself or anyone around me, but I was refusing to acknowledge that, either. It was just frustrating.

"I don't know who I am." I looked away from him. "I'm not one way, and I'm not another, so I don't know *what* I am!"

"And that's why you're so confused." Jordan reached out and gently turned me back around to face him again. "You think it has to be either this way or that way." He was desperate to get me to understand what he was saying. "Don't you get it? There is no this or that! There's only you, and then everybody else."

"I don't want to be like everybody else," I countered.

"You don't have to be." Jordan spoke very softly

now. "Why should you have to stop being who you are? Why should you lose your own identity to become like what you see in your mind as everybody else? Don't you think that others would benefit from who *you* are, what *you* have to say and how *you* choose to say it?"

"It hurts to be me." I was beginning to choke up.

"You think it doesn't hurt to be me? Remember JR? Do you think I'm proud of that?" He looked disgusted just talking about his ex, so I gathered not. "But that's life. We live and learn, but at least I'm out there trying and I'm going to learn by my mistakes. Why should you get off scot-free while the rest of us have to suffer through this?"

"Because I'm better off alone."

"You might think you've got it made by yourself, but when those people who are suffering now eventually find happiness in another human being, regardless if it's a man or a woman, you're still going to be at the starting line wondering how they got so far ahead of you. Worse yet, you won't understand what they have, and you'll still be lonely, still be needing. If you have a chance to find happiness, why not take it? Whatever it is...or whoever."

"Because I don't want to be different!" I screamed, and we both jumped. "Let me tell you something about different—it sucks." I started to shake. "I went to grade school with a kid who was different. He played with dolls and acted more feminine than what was accepted or considered normal in adolescence. Everybody teased him, including me, and it never stopped, not even in high school. In fact, it got worse." I grimaced. "It disgusts me to even think about because I was part of the problem.

"Hell, I helped *perpetuate* the problem by never trying to understand what he instinctively knew and accepted about himself. There's no doubt in my mind that he was and is to this day gay, but that's who I saw in my early years and what I equated all gays to be like. They acted like him, and everybody else reacted like we did."

Jordan didn't say a word. I was hoping he would stop me, tell me that I hadn't done anything wrong because I just didn't know any better back then; but that didn't excuse how I had been acting lately, and he remained silent. How ironic it seemed at this moment that I had been so willfully ignorant in the past and didn't seem to be doing much to improve it lately.

"I never defended him," I continued, "and I detest myself for that. There were opportunities to help him out, but I took advantage of them to fit in with a much larger crowd who didn't accept me any more then they did him. When I graduated, all I could think about was getting away from them and never looking back. Maybe I couldn't change the past, but I could have at least told him that I was sorry, and I didn't even do that. Instead, I just left and brought the ghosts and problems with me."

"Problems?" he asked softly.

I don't think I knew another human being I could have had this conversation with. Yes, I had problems, only I had never admitted them before. My defenses had stopped that from happening for years, and now I was being confronted by the absolute worst thing a human can be confronted with—himself.

The cards were all on the table. Only the truths of the hand dealt to me from birth were there to be read. No more cunning bluffs. No more lies.

"I never did apologize to you the other day when I said all those things about gays. You were right. I was—am—ignorant, and I've been very cruel to you, even tonight. I'm sorry."

He started to say something, but I raised my hand to let him know I wasn't done. If I didn't say these things now, I might never.

"I also lied to you that first night about having slept with all those women. The only naked women I've ever seen were back in grade school in *National Geographic* and they were spreading the wings of insects they were going to eat for a snack, not their legs for me to pleasure myself in. I've never had sex...with a partner, anyway. I wouldn't even know how to attract someone."

"You wouldn't know how?" Jordan looked at me as if I'd spoken gibberish. "Excuse me? That boy, Nate, really liked you tonight. I feel sorry for him, because he's going to be taking cold showers for the next month."

"Please, don't...don't joke right now." I fought back a pain in the pit of my stomach. "There's something else I have to tell you. God, this...I don't know how...I've been lying to myself for a long time now. I think I just finally ran out of ways to justify my efforts to keep myself quiet." Tears welled up in my eyes. "It's supposed to be wrong, morally and religiously, yet I can't quote scripture supporting that argument to save my life. It's supposed to be a choice, yet I know it's not a choice."

I looked past Jordan—through him, maybe, and into my past. "It couldn't be, not with what I know and how I feel, how I've never stopped feeling it.

"The only conscious choice I made," I continued, "was to do absolutely nothing about it. It was never safe to confront myself before, and it's not now, but it's who I really am. When I was slow-dancing with Nate tonight..."

Jordan's gaze dropped for a moment, and I knew he was expecting me to tell him that I'd felt something for my dance partner.

"...the only arms I wanted to be in were yours."

His eyes rose up and met mine.

"I wanted so badly for you to be jealous when I was with Nate that I became someone I didn't like. I didn't have the courage to tell you how I'd started to feel. How could I? I never even had the courage to admit to myself that..."

Here it was at long last.

"I'm gay." It felt both terrifying and liberating to say, so I said it again. "I'm gay."

"Come here." Jordan moved closer and gave me a hug.

Perhaps it was the simplest form of expression in the world, but it made all the difference in my world right then. The tears I'd been holding back began to flow, and I was soon sobbing like someone who's just had the weight of the world lifted from his shoulders.

"I want you to know that I understand how you feel right now. You've taken a big step in life. and the first is always the hardest." He held me tighter. I didn't care if he talked or not because I felt safe for the moment, safer than I'd ever felt before. "It's going to be okay.

"I've known my entire life that I'm gay," he continued and shuddered, no doubt remembering his own ghosts. "I never told anybody. It felt so natural for me that I never really thought to tell anyone.

"When I got into high school and saw how people who felt like I did were treated, I decided I couldn't stay quiet anymore. It wasn't fair, but I was too naive to realize that it was never *going* to be fair. I sat both my parents down one night not long after and told them the truth about what I am...about *who* I am."

"What happened?" I was finally calming down enough to talk without making all sorts of strange noises. "What did they say?"

I looked at him through blurred eyes. Had they hurt him? Disowned him? It must have been bad for him to leave and not go back or ask for help when things got rough.

"It's not important because this isn't about me. It's about you. I just want you to know that you aren't alone and that things will work out."

If there was any pain in his past, not a single trace of it showed in his expression, at least that I could see. He wasn't going to tell me—if there was anything to tell at all.

"Now I want to ask you something."

I didn't know what he could possibly have to ask. There was nothing left of my life that was much of a secret, and even if there was, I doubt I could take the stress of unearthing any more of my ghosts tonight.

"What you said about dancing with Nate and all?

Maybe you're going to think I'm a little arrogant, but you've been hot for me from the start, right? You were just playing hard to get?"

"What?" I pushed him away from me. A *little* arrogant? "I go through one of the most traumatic experiences of my life..." I took a step towards him, and he took a step back. "...and all you can think of is whether or not I'm *hot* for you?" We repeated the step thing again. "I bare my *soul* to you, and all you can wonder is if I've been *playing hard to get?*"

"No." He took one more step back. "I also wondered if I'd get a chance to see that ass of yours that seems to have impressed so many people." He wiggled his eyebrows up and down several times. "Does that count?"

"*You are so dead!*" I started for him, and he bolted out of the room.

Jordan didn't have much of a head start, so I ended up easily cornering him in the living room. The infuriating part of this was that he was fast, much faster than I was. Just when I thought he couldn't escape, he made a mad dash for the hallway and to the bedroom at the end of it. While it was a clear shot for him, the couch blocked my way. I wasn't about to let that stop me, however. I used it to my advantage and, yelling a war cry, simply launched myself off the end of it and tackled him before he made it to safety.

He was too stunned to resist when I rolled him over and held his hands down. I was just starting to gloat when he recovered, brought his legs up and knocked me off-balance. Next thing I knew, we were rolling around trying to see which one of us could get the upper hand.

It wasn't much of a struggle because by this time we were both laughing too hard to put up much of a fight. We ended up in the same position we had been in at the beach, his arms wrapped tightly around my neck, only there wasn't any water under us. Jordan didn't have to worry about being dunked, and I didn't have to worry about keeping his head up as well as my own.

Maybe he planned it this way, but my strength was about gone and I had to lower myself before I collapsed. I didn't want his head to bounce on the ground, so I went down slowly and gently. I expected him to release me once he was safely flat on the floor and then let me fall to the side. That didn't happen, though, and I ended up directly on top of him.

My chest was on his, and I could feel the heat of his body. Something stirred inside me; my heart skipped a few beats then sped up. I looked down at him then, my face surely echoing my mass confusion, and closed my eyes.

A few seconds passed, but it felt like an eternity. It wasn't because it was awkward; rather, it was because I was taking everything in that I possibly could about him—the heat from his body, the smell of his cologne, the feel of his breath on my face. My heart was pounding so hard I thought it was going to come right out of my chest.

I was about to rest my chin on his shoulder, to be that much closer to him, when he let go from around my neck.

"We've been here before," he whispered.

"Not like this." I knew what he was doing, but I didn't want it to end. After all the grief I'd given him, and even after I'd told him that I was gay, he was still giving me a way out. If only I could get up the nerve to do what I wanted to. "Not like this," I repeated and opened my eyes.

"Maybe we should get up, and I'll make us some popcorn or…"

"Why don't you shut up." It was now or never! I lowered my head and very lightly touched my lips to his. It was his turn to have the bulging-eye look, and he didn't seem in any hurry to return the gesture. Why?

"Please…you don't have to do that. You don't owe me anything," he assured me. "I don't want you doing this for the wrong reasons."

"Jordan." I sighed. "I've been thinking about this since I first met you. I was just too stupid to admit and act on it."

He tried to say something else, but I put a finger on his lips.

"It's very difficult for me to admit to someone how I feel inside, how I really feel. Remember that whole safe-bet thing? So, please, don't give me a hard time when I tell you that I'm trying to meet you halfway. You've shared so much with me, and I've shared so little. Let me do this not because I feel I have to, but because I want to."

"Okay."

"Do you still feel the same way about me, like you did on the night we met?" I could feel his own heart racing, and it made me feel a little better to know I wasn't in this alone. I also felt something else, so I was sure this was one of those safe-bet things I liked so much.

"Uh…" Jordan suddenly seemed to be having a

difficult time concentrating on what I was saying. "You're teasing me, aren't you? I mean, this time you're really teasing...as a payback for what I said to you in the kitchen, right? If this is some kind of a joke..."

"I don't really know what I'm supposed to do or what I'm supposed to be thinking about doing." I sat up and looked down at him. "If the incident in the bathroom at the club tonight is any indication, we could be in real trouble. All I do know, all I feel, is that I want to be with you. I want this. How about you?"

"Bathroom?"

I gave him a look that told him it was a story for another time.

"Well." The sparkle slowly began to return to his eyes. "I don't think you have to worry about my intentions because, whatever happens, I'm sure you won't be needing this."

He reached up and helped me out of my T-shirt. The little tease just couldn't resist letting his fingertips slide gently down my chest, making me tremble almost uncontrollably. Nobody had ever given me that sensation before.

I felt very exposed and very vulnerable. It wasn't like we were at the beach and expected to walk around without a shirt. Guys took their shirts off. It was their function in life, especially when at the beach. They didn't touch each other the way he was touching me, but I'm sure they noticed each other in some way. Now...

Now I was being noticed not as just some guy without his shirt, but as some guy who someone was physically attracted to without his shirt. It made me feel uncomfortable. It made me feel exposed. It made me feel...

Jordan took his own shirt off.

"Oh, my God!" I couldn't stop staring at his body. It took some of the pressure off me, and I didn't feel so exposed anymore. Actually, I was starting to like this whole naked chest thing.

"Get down here." He laughed lightly and pulled me down on top of him, chest to chest, and kissed me.

I'd never really kissed anybody before. Well, at least, not like this. It was a strange sensation, but...wow! Hot!

We started off with just the light brushing of the lips and maybe an occasional lingering moment before separating. Then I became a little more daring, and he met my curiosity with his own kind of satisfaction. Before long, it was like taking a drink of the best elixir known to man, in long, deep gulps. Sure, it sounds corny, but I didn't know any other way to describe it. It's not like I had other experiences to compare it to, so it was perfect, even in its corniness. My only fear was that, since my heart was still beating several thousands of miles a minute and I was sweating, I would start drooling and some of it would accidentally slide down into his mouth.

"Wow." Jordan used his hands to guide me off him, and we stood up. He took my hand and led me down the hall. So, this is how it happened. There didn't have to be any fancy lines, no bullshit about what state or city I lived in, what school I went to, what income bracket I fell into or what my occupation was. This really could take place between two people who liked the look of each other, enjoyed some intellectual stimulation and were of the same sex. Color me happy!

We didn't quite end up in the bedroom, though. He instead steered us into the bathroom and turned on the light.

"Here?" What was the fascination gay men had with bathrooms anyway?

"After dancing and sweating for most of the night, we could both use a shower."

He had a point, yet I thought sweating was a part of something we were going to be doing anyway. Still, cleanliness was a good idea.

He turned on the water and, when it was finally warm, turned the faucet to shower.

"Ready?" When I didn't move, he reached over and started to undo the button of my shorts.

"Uh..." I had to think of something quick. "I'm sort of...you know...up at the moment." As if he couldn't tell.

"That's okay. So am I."

He finished undoing my button, pulled the zipper down and then the shorts altogether. I must have looked like a complete idiot standing there in my underwear with an erection the size of...

Well, I never bothered to measure it, but it was damn noticeable even if I do say so myself. It was even more so when he gently pulled my underwear down and let them fall to the floor on top of the shorts.

If I'd ever felt naked before, I definitely was the epitome of it now. All I could do was stand there and remember to breathe so I didn't have a heart attack. That is, until he reached up and guided my hands to the button on *his* shorts.

I worked carefully and quickly on them. and they were soon down on the floor with my own. All I had to do now was remove his underwear.

They slid to the ground.

"Oh, my God." Diane's suspicions about his "package" were dead on!

"Do you smell aloe?" he asked, sniffing.

"Yeah, I used it earlier on my..." No. I really didn't want to divulge that. It was one thing to admit one's sexuality, but quite another to mention what one did with one's privates. "Hold that thought."

We stepped into the shower and took turns rinsing off. I knew he was watching me, but when I turned around to wipe the water from my eyes, I saw that he was kneeling down in front of me. An image came readily to mind, and I started to panic.

"What are you doing?" I asked a little too quickly.

"Don't get excited." He couldn't help but chuckle at what I must be thinking was going on. "The soap slipped out of my hand, and I was picking it up."

"Sorry." I felt really stupid.

"Don't be."

He took the bar of soap and started running it along my chest and down my arms. I hadn't had someone bathe me since I was in diapers, and I hadn't expected to have someone do it again until I was in diapers once more.

It was soon my turn to soap him up. Jordan was excited, that was quite obvious, but he gave off an air of calm that helped me get through the more interesting parts of our cleansing. There were a couple of close calls, and considering how our bodies reacted to each other, it was a good thing he had never been in one of my gym classes at school or been my roommate this past year at college. I'd have been on academic probation for two semesters because I'd never have gone to class.

We dried off, picked our clothes up and went into the bedroom. I closed and locked the door just to be on the safe side. The last thing I wanted was to have Jenny and Kenny come home unexpectedly and decide to check up on us. Knowing them, though, they'd probably congratulate us both.

Jordan hadn't turned on the light, and I assumed we were going to keep it off, but I was having a difficult time seeing where I was going.

"Are you okay?" Jordan asked from across the room.

"Yeah, just keep talking." I laughed nervously. "I know my suitcase is somewhere around here and..." Smack! "Shit. Found it. Are you on the top or bottom bunk?"

"Bottom. Just be sure to watch your..." Thud! "...head."

"Owwwww," I moaned, "that's going to leave a mark."

"I seem to keep asking this," he sat up and wrapped his arms around my waist, "but are you okay?"

"I'm fine. You'd think I was masochistic the way I beat myself up sometimes."

I took his hands, and he guided me down onto the bed next to him.

"I know I told you this earlier, but I feel like I should tell you again. I really don't know what I'm doing. I don't want you to think I'm not interested

239

because I am, but..." My voice trailed off. This was one of those times when I was talking too much.

"Would you mind if I went ahead and took the lead, then?"

"I was kind of hoping you would." I felt as if some of the pressure was off me now. At least he understood.

"Anything that you don't feel comfortable with, just say something. We'll take it slow."

"Jordan?"

"Yeah."

"Would you please just shut up?"

He laughed a bit as he leaned over and kissed my neck, producing an entirely new sensation. He stopped a moment later, and I heard him opening one of the drawers on the dresser next to the bed. It sounded like he brought something out, but I couldn't see what it was.

"What's that?"

"A few things..." He closed the drawer. "...we'll need a little later. How do you feel?"

"Like a flag at full mast."

"That's about right." He made good on his word and took the initiative. Tenderly, he wrapped me in his arms and pulled me over on top of him. "And now?"

"If you keep up generating all these sensations I'm feeling, you're going to find out a whole lot sooner than I think we'd both like."

"In that case..." I heard him reach over to where he'd placed whatever he'd taken out of the dresser. "...we'd better use some of this and one of these." A few moments passed. "There. How does that feel?"

"Oh, my God!"

9

I couldn't remember dreaming anything much that night. What could I possibly dream about when everything my dreams had been pointing to had come true? We held each other the entire night, even rolling over at the same time when one of us needed to change position. Sometimes Jordan was wrapped up in my arms and sometimes I was in his.

When I finally opened my eyes the next morning, I found myself in his arms. It was the best way I think I've ever woken up in my life. His chin rested on my shoulder, and I could feel his breath on my bare skin. I, on the other hand, was resting my face on his chest and feeling the gentle rise and fall. Despite the raging it created in my hormones, I couldn't remember a more peaceful and contented moment.

"Are you awake?" he whispered.

"Me and my anatomy." Just the sound of his voice was enough to do that now. "I have to ask you something."

"Yes, it was as good for me. Also, yes, I did peek

at your ass in the shower and it exceeds its reputation."

"That wasn't what I was going to ask, but thanks for sharing." I didn't want this to be a typical "morning after" like was so often seen in the movies or read in cheap novels. "I used to try and tell myself that sex was supposed to be free, given out on a plate and gorged, only I never could find out for myself no matter how hard I tried. A deeper part of me wanted to hold on to tradition, though, and save that experience for someone I fell in love with and who was in love with me."

"Andy," Jordan soothed.

"I know we're not in love with each other. I haven't been here very long and I'm leaving tomorrow." I fought back a lump in my throat. "But I want you to know, if I was going to be here, going to school or spending the entire summer..." My voice started to waver. "I think I would fall in love with you."

He pulled me closer to him.

"I knew last night that I was going to have to leave, but I didn't care," I went on. "Does that make what we did wrong? Does it make me a bad person for wanting you anyway?"

"No, it doesn't." Jordan turned me over to face him. "It takes two willing people to do what we did last night. If there's any guilt to be handed out, it would have to be to me for starting this at the anniversary party. I may have made you face something you weren't ready to yet, and I don't know what the consequences will be for you." He put his hand on my chest. "And if you were going to be here for a while, I think I'd fall in love with you, too."

"Really?"

"Really." He leaned down to kiss me, but I stopped him. "What? You don't believe me?"

"No." I turned away. "You just have really bad morning breath." I couldn't keep a straight face.

"Oh, really?" Jordan attempted to look indignant. "Well, yours isn't exactly roses, either." He tried to push me off the bed, but I held on.

"They made you leave, didn't they?"

He stopped his playful assault, and I think I saw tears start to form in his eyes.

"For whatever reason, your parents wouldn't kick you out, so they made things bad enough to make you want to leave on your own, right?"

Based on what little he'd told me, it was the only thing that made sense.

"Is it really that important for you to know?"

It was. I'm nosy. It runs in the family.

"No son of my parents was born a 'cocksucking faggot.' In their eyes, it's a choice, and since I made the choice to be that way, I could just as easily make the choice not to be." Jordan was fighting his emotions, but tears started to stream down his face. "I became a thing to them, an example of how not to let your children grow up, and finally, an endless source of shame. There was no way I could give them what they wanted in a son, so I left and stopped them from having to worry about me at all.

"Aunt Jenny let them know when I moved here, but they've never called or asked about me and I've never called them, either. The only one I've had any contact with is my sister, and she told me they don't even acknowledge anymore that they've got a son. They took down all my pictures, threw out all of my belongings and won't discuss me under any circumstance. I've never gone back, and I never will."

The tears flowed freely now, and he collapsed in my arms.

"It's all right." I soothed him and ran my hands through his hair. "It sounds like we're both going to be in therapy for a long time."

Jordan managed a weak laugh. If he only knew what I was scheming. The conversation had grown too serious, and it was now my turn to build a false sense of security then drop some smartass comment when he was least expecting it. After his "you want me, don't you" comment last night, it was the least I could do.

"It's a shame your parents will never know how much they're missing out on. Hell, my life was perfectly fine until you practically stuck your tongue down my throat several nights ago."

He froze.

"I mean, you're a real bundle of fucking joy to be around."

He looked at me, eyes narrowing and aware of exactly what I was doing.

"Sexual innuendoes, public embarrassment, sand up the crack of my ass, watching you hump somebody's leg as you danced at a gay club, nearly getting me accosted by an old boyfriend and then, last night, putting my..."

"You're going down!" Jordan wrapped his arms around my body and pulled me over the side of the bed with him. I was laughing too hard to put up much of a fight.

"I didn't get to finish telling you about last night." I mimicked pouting.

"Maybe I don't want to be reminded." He rolled over on top of me.

"Maybe I already forgot because it wasn't that memorable." I tried to keep a straight face, but ended up laughing at my own joke. "Okay, so I'm lying. It was very memorable. And...hey!" My comments were stirring more than his memory. "When did that wake up?" I teased.

"I think about the same time you mentioned humping somebody's leg."

"Will you bark like a dog for me?" I teased. "God knows you salivate like one."

"Really?" Jordan feigned being hurt. "You're so cruel. In fact, you're so cruel I think it's time I gave you some obedience training!"

I wrapped my arms around him and held him close. If last night was any indication of what I was in for this morning, then I doubted he could call it obedience training, not when the pupil was this willing to please.

🌿 🌿 🌿

The rest of the day flew by. Jenny and Kenny came home before long—or what seemed to me before long—and started talking about where to go out for dinner. Diane dropped the kids off shortly after that, and it was decided we would all go out somewhere special to celebrate my last night.

I think they suspected something had happened because there were several remarks made about how I must have gotten some sun at the beach to be glowing like I was. Even Diane made mention of how I was smiling a whole lot more than she remembered me doing before.

She also mentioned I was walking funny, like I'd been out riding a horse. If she only knew. Oh, hell! They probably all knew damn well what had happened, only they were just being nice about it.

Jenny even gave me a compliment on how well I'd made my bed when she went to change the sheets. Of course, she knew the damn thing hadn't been slept in, but it was all their way of telling us it was fine by them and our business.

Grandma called later that afternoon to make arrangements for her and Aunt Virginia to pick me up in the morning on the way to the airport. Uncle Chester wouldn't be joining us, though. He'd apparently always had a severe case of arachnophobia and had reached under his pillow two nights ago to discover he had squashed one of the largest spiders he'd ever laid eyes on. His doctors said the tranquilizers they had him on were doing their job and that he could come home in another day.

I wasn't particularly thrilled about leaving, but I knew I couldn't stay. There was a life waiting for me back in Michigan, a life I would have to work on gradually to change into the person I now knew myself to be. I had my work cut out for me.

Jordan wasn't happy about me leaving so soon, either, but he put on a damn good show of strength. It was such an unusual occurrence to see someone go through so much effort for me. He even managed to arrange one final walk at the beach to see the stars that night, and just when I thought the last of the surprises had come to an end, he produced two tiny bottles of champagne and we toasted our final evening together. I didn't know where this fondness and affection for me came from, or if I even deserved it, but I was bound and determined to live in the moment and enjoy it.

After we got back home, Jordan insisted we have each other's addresses and phone numbers, and we promised to use them. Maybe we couldn't be lovers, but we could be friends; and that's what really counted in the long run. Of course, it didn't stop us from pretending to be lovers again that night...all night.

❧ ❧ ❧

The feeling of orgasmic euphoria I'd come to love so much when a plane took off seemed to have lost its luster. There was still a bit of a rush, but not nearly like what I'd experienced in the past two days, not even close.

Grandma sat next to me gripping a freshly opened mini-bottle of scotch in one hand and a bottle of whiskey in the other. She hadn't said too much since picking me up this morning, but I could tell she'd had a good couple of days. Much of that was probably due to spending all her time with Aunt Virginia and not her instigating brother. Whether or not she'd remember it after waking up with Roberto tomorrow morning was an entirely different matter. It might all have been a dream.

Either way, I was pretty certain Grandma wasn't going to say anything to my parents about me taking off and not doing any work. They'd laugh at her if she did. I know I would.

"What are you thinking about?" she asked, noticing an expression on my face she didn't recognize—contentment.

"Nothing."

I had asked Jordan just before I left the house if what we had shared could possibly ever be any better. I couldn't imagine it with anyone else, and I wasn't sure I wanted to. He thought that was incredibly sweet, then grew very serious and peered directly into my eyes, maybe into my soul.

"One of these days, you'll fall in love with someone who won't be able to help but fall in love with you, too. You'll give him the world and never think twice about it. You'll never look back, and I'll be insanely jealous but happy that I've been a part of your life and you mine. We'll always have that. And if you ever need me, I'll be there."

He was so Michael Paré in *Streets of Fire*.

We gave each other a farewell kiss, something I'd actually grown to enjoy; then I went out to make my goodbyes to the rest of the family. Grandma ushered me off shortly after.

"Nothing?" She was practically slurring. "You look like you got too much sun. You're makin' my eyes hurt the way you're glowing."

"Well..." I looked over at her. "I was thinking about Alphaville. They have a song about believing in dreams. I was just thinking how true those lyrics are."

My adventure in life was just beginning. Maybe I'd write about it as it happened. Then again, who'd believe it?

"More of your generation's music." She looked away in disgust. "Whatever happened to Frank Sinatra? Whatever happened to Bing Crosby?"

"They fossilized." I pulled out a Kleenex. "Wipe your chin, Grandma. You're drooling again."

And with that, I left California.

Forever changed...

END

ABOUT THE AUTHOR

KAGE ALAN grew up in a suburb of Detroit, Michigan, the Motor City—and, if you think about it, the only state where someone can hold their hand up and point to where they live. He attended Grand Valley State University in Allendale, the really, really quiet city, and graduated with a BA in Creative Writing and Film & Video. He has since returned to the aforementioned suburb of Detroit, where he resides with his previously unmentioned half-Asian and wholly domineering partner.

Kage enjoys buying DVDs, traveling overseas (and buying DVDs there), eating sushi, fibbing to his partner about that DVDs he may or may not have picked up that week, playing Laser Tag, attending sci-fi conventions and allowing the everyday goofy behavior of himself and those around him to inspire his writing. He can otherwise be found via email at Kage24@aol.com and online at www.myspace/kagealan.

ABOUT THE ARTIST

ANGELA WATERS's eclectic tastes in music and books have converged with her fascination with technology. Sleepless nights are filled with listening to hardcore rockers and playing out the tunes in colors that describe her vision of an author's words. Her muse is thrilled it finally has a place to cut loose.

Printed in the United States
216354BV00001B/25/P